# TWO-MOONS AND
# THE BLACK TOWER

## Borgo Press Books by Ardath Mayhar

*The Absolutely Perfect Horse: A Novel of East Texas* (with Marylois Dunn)
*The Body in the Swamp: An Occult Mystery*
*Carrots and Miggle: A Novel of East Texas*
*The Clarrington Heritage*
*Closely Knit in Scarlatt*
*Crazy Quilt: The Best Short Stories of Ardath Mayhar*
*Deadly Memoir: A Novel of Suspense*
*Death in the Square*
*The Door in the Hill: A Tale of the Turnipins*
*The Dropouts: A Tale of Growing Up in East Texas*
*Feud at Sweetwater Creek: A Novel of the Old West*
*The Fugitives: A Tale of Prehistoric Times*
*The Heirs of Three Oaks: A Novel of the Old West*
*High Mountain Winter: A Novel of the Old West*
*How the Gods Wove in Kyrannon: Tales of the Triple Moons*
*Hunters of the Plains: A Novel of Prehistoric America*
*Island in the Lake: A Novel of Native America*
*Khi to Freedom: A Science Fiction Novel*
*The Lintons of Skillet Bend: A Novel of East Texas*
*Lone Runner: A Novel of the Old West*
*Lords of the Triple Moons: A Science Fantasy Novel: Tales of the Triple Moons*
*Makra Choria: A Novel of High Fantasy*
*Medicine Dream: Being the Further Adventures of Burr Henderson*
*Messengers in White: A Science Fantasy Novel*
*Monkey Station: A Novel of the Future* (Macaque Cycle #1; with Ron Fortier)
*People of the Mesa: A Novel of Native America*
*A Planet Called Heaven: A Science Fiction Novel*
*Prescription for Danger: A Novel of the Old West*
*Reflections; & Journey to an Ending: Collected Poems*
*A Road of Stars: A Fantasy of Life, Death, Love, and Art*
*Runes of the Lyre: A Science Fantasy Novel*
*The Saga of Grittel Sundotha: A Science Fantasy Novel*
*The Seekers of Shar-Nuhn: Tales of the Triple Moons*
*Shock Treatment: An Account of Granary's War*
*Slewfoot Sally and the Flying Mule: Tall Tales from Cotton County, Texas*
*Soul-Singer of Tyrnos: A Fantasy Novel*
*Strange Doings in the Pine Hills: Stories*
*Through a Stone Wall: Lessons from Thirty Years of Writing*
*Timber Pirates: A Novel of East Texas* (with Marylois Dunn)
*Towers of the Earth: A Novel of Native America*
*Trail of the Seahawks: A Novel of the Future* (Macaque Cycle #2; with R. Fortier)
*The Tulpa: A Novel of Fantasy*
*Two-Moons and the Black Tower: A Novel of Fantasy*
*Vendetta*
*Warlock's Gift: Tales of the Triple Moons*
*The World Ends in Hickory Hollow: A Novel of the Future*
*A World of Weirdities: Tales to Shiver By*

# TWO-MOONS AND THE BLACK TOWER

## A Novel of Fantasy

by

**Ardath Mayhar**

### THE BORGO PRESS

*An Imprint of Wildside Press LLC*

**MMIX**

# CONTENTS

# FOREWORD

One dreary day I was sitting in my living room, reading a book about the Iroquoian tribes. I looked up, and onto the TV screen came an ad (can't recall what it advertised) which showed a dark tower standing on an island and surrounded by snow. At that instant, this book popped into my head. Not that I knew what would happen—if I did, I would have no reason to write the book. The story was intensely interesting to write, and I hope you find it as interesting to read.

—Ardath Mayhar
Chireno, Texas
October 2008

# CHAPTER ONE

## THE BLACK TOWER

Two-Moons struggled beneath the weight of the deer on her back. It was beginning to tell upon her strength, though the effort of carrying it helped, to some extent, to counteract the terrible chill of the evening. A blizzard howled among the great trees about her, as if all the wolves in the country of her people had come there after prey, and Two-Moons had begun to wonder if this hunt might be her last.

She would not hesitate to go into death, she thought. Being the provider for her family was not easy, for other women often derided her for becoming a warrior and hunter. That had been her fate, however, for her mother had taken the same path, though she had no sisters to keep her household in order.

A widow with three young daughters, she had taken bow and spear and mastered them, though the tribe would have cared for them all in the longhouse, as it did other bereft families. Yet her mother was too proud and independent to take from others, and the women of the tribe, even then, had not liked her ways. It had been the truth of her dreams that allowed her the choice, for the People lived by dreams, those messages sent by the spirits to guide them.

A gust of snow-laden wind whipped into the woman's face, almost choking her. She paused to lean against a huge elm, easing her burden on her aching shoulders. Shifting her bow to a better position, she stood still in the snow-light, listening intently.

In the distance she could hear a dog bark. There lay the longhouse where her sisters waited with her bearskin bedding warmed, and strips of meat for her last meal sputtering into the coals. Soon she would be there, sheltered from the storm.

She straightened and trudged on, guided by her instinct, for the path and the forest were invisible, hidden by fresh swirls of snow.

The warmth of the deer carcass against her back had chilled, now, and she longed to be at home again. Not for the first time she wondered why she and her mother had been chosen for such difficult lives.

Her friend Runs-Bucks-Down could have made this journey, even burdened with meat, much more quickly on his long legs. Why had she not accepted his offer to move into her part of the longhouse? Life would be easier, if she were a woman, at least in winter, though summer would have found her digging in her cornfields and dressing out skins and meat.

She sighed and hefted the carcass again. That sort of thought sometimes intruded when she was doing something beyond her size and almost beyond her strength. Yet one who dreamed truly could not be content to farm, work hides, do all the routine tasks that others were better suited for. That would ruin her ability, for her dreams nourished and protected the spirit of the tribe, as did those of the other dreamers. For some strange reason, the Master of Life had given to her mother's line a great deal of orenda. Life-spirit must not be wasted, and those yoked to dull routine did not dream truly.

Two-Moons realized that something had changed while she rested. The wind seemed less sharp than it had been. The snow was settling, and she could see farther into the distance. The bite of the snow-smell in her nostrils seemed subtly different as well.

She raised her head and sniffed. The underlying odor of the forest beneath the snow seemed different, too. She stared hard at the bole of a huge tree just ahead. Outlined in black against the snow, it had a strange shape, alien to her eyes.

Stepping forward, she laid her numbed hand against the bark. It seemed to be an oak, but its texture was subtly different from those she knew. There was, besides, no oak this large between the edge of the lake and the longhouse for which she was bound. Her people knew the trees of the forest as intimately as they knew the members of the tribe, and this was no tree she had ever met before.

Huddled against that alien tree, she listened hard. She could not hear the bark of the dog now. Silence wrapped the forest. She pushed herself up again, knowing that some demon spirit, some false-face must be seeking to mislead her.

She knew that the home of her people lay ahead, and she must go there or make camp. It was too cold to continue trudging through the snow, and surviving without shelter was not likely. She thought of her warm bearskin beside the fire and stumbled forward, finding no path flattening the soil beneath the snow. Only rough drifts covering deadfall seemed to lie all about her.

Before long she realized that something was wrong; she should have reached the Onondaga village by now, for she was moving as quickly as possible in the deep snow. Yet now she stood beside an ice-locked stream whose gurgle could be heard beneath its frosting of snow. There should be no stream here. Had she become confused in her struggle through the dim forest?

The snow thinned and stopped; the wan light of that covering the ground made the forest seem even dimmer, etched with the shapes of thick trunks and tangled

10

branches. The shapes seemed oak-like, but very ancient oaks swollen with years. Here, so near the village, should be a stand of elm and maple.

Hitching the deer higher on her back, she stepped forward, knowing that there might be no shelter tonight. She might have to build a brush hut, in order to survive the chill. Still, she did not pause, not yet. Something lay before her, and her dream-trained sense felt it calling to her. She must see what lay ahead.

Her feet found a trail—not a game trail, like that she had been following, but a regular path made by human feet, wide and hard-packed beneath the snow. Even through her moccasins she could feel the surface. She could also see something through the veiling branches and the dim twilight. When she emerged into the open, she paused, her mouth open, staring upward. It seemed that some mad tribe had built a longhouse but had set it on end, rather than laying it sensibly along the earth. The shape was black against the slightly paler sky, and it stood in the middle of a larger stream, a small river indeed.

She could see the darkness at its foot and knew it stood on an island, now connected to the land by ice much thicker than she expected it to be. Even as she stared, a flicker of ruddy light winked from an opening high in the side of the strange shelter.

She studied the shape, squinting to penetrate the dimness. There was no door-flap that she could see, even as she drew nearer, crossing the ice cautiously after she deposited her deer on the path. Once she was at the foot of the shelter, she touched it, finding it made of unyielding stone. How had anyone piled it so high? And what kept it from falling down?

Fumbling around the foot of the thing, Two-Moons found no yielding skin flap, although there were many cracks and crannies that ran in straight lines, up and down or across the surface.

She backed away and looked across the river. There was forest beyond the pale line of the stream and the white line of snow marking the path. She moved back over the ice to the spot where she left her meat. It seemed she might need that deer carcass, before she found her way home again.

Moving deep into the fringe of trees, she fashioned a crude shelter of brush, cutting her building material from thick growth that would not show the missing branches. She piled the brush carefully, hiding the structure in a thicket of bramble and holly that filled a small glade in the wood. Thankful for her kill earlier that evening, she cut off a haunch, already half frozen, and piled more brush over the rest of the deer. Once inside her shelter she carved thin strips from the haunch and chewed them slowly, savoring the bloody juices. Meat was strength and warmth, and she must keep herself fueled for whatever dangers she might meet in this strange dream-place.

Her outer robe was buckskin, tanned finely by her sister Laughs-Too-Much. She tucked her arms inside that, when she was ready to rest, protecting them between that and her inner shirt, which was made of beaver fur. Sitting with her back against a springy wall, her legs crossed, spine straight, she prepared to call upon Aireskoi for aid, as her people did at need. She began to sing a quavering tune, very softly to avoid attracting unwanted attention in this unfamiliar country.

> Aireskoi, who guides the hunt,
> who strengthens the arm in warfare,
> who sends the sun to warm the lands,
> that crops and game may flourish,
> to you I make my song.
> There is need of a dream,
> a true vision.
> I, the daughter of Dreams-True,

12

ask this of you.

Her song had many verses, for she did not know if Ai-reskoi lived in this place. If he were far away, there was need for a long, long song to find him and bring him here. When she finished, she sat with her eyes closed, resting and waiting. But it was not a dream or a vision that approached her at last. There came the crunch of human footsteps in new snow.

In an instant, she was outside, hidden amid the thicket, her knife in hand. Slipping to the edge of the stream, she concealed herself amid the shadows of leafless willow trees and bushes, where the dark blot of her shape against the snow would not be distinguishable from that of a clump of reeds or a bush.

Her bow and arrows were behind her shoulder, fastened to their thong, but she did not know, as yet, if this might be an enemy. In this alien place, she might well need a friend, if this might prove to be one. She worked her arms free, flexed her fingers and gripped the knife afresh. Then she crouched, silent and waiting, to see who came toward her across the snow-laden ice of the stream.

The shape was only a dark blot at first, but it was taller than anyone among her own people. Some sort of loose robe flapped about it, moved by the breeze of its passing. Two-Moons hugged a dense bush and watched intently as the shape took the path she had followed into the wood. The snow-light was stronger, and she could now see him.

Breath froze in her throat. The face was white—whiter even than that of a False-Face in the trees of her Onondaga forest. It shone between the dark stuff of the robe and a black hood that covered the head.

Two-Moons had never encountered the False-Face herself, although her mother had died after encountering one of those disembodied heads.

She had spoken of the terror of it with her last breath.

Was this such a being? Then she rejected the notion. This one had a body, though it was too tall and thin to be quite human.

She caught her breath, finding in her heart a question. Did this creature possess orenda? That was the spirit-stuff that bound all things together, man and beast, plant and water and air. All things of the world were a part of it, as it was a part of them. Yet was this being a part of the world she knew? She found it in her heart to doubt that. Still....

She inhaled silently and deeply, letting her spirit walk forth a bit to test and taste the spirits of the things around her. Strong, bitter spirits inhabited the oaks, which muttered among themselves about men like these, who slaughtered their sister trees and burned them. The bushes had a lighter, sweeter flavor, for they were in no danger from Men, except for the pilfering fingers of children among the summer berries.

All the grasses were asleep. The water was frozen to considerable depth, stilling its voice. The air was still busy with the memory of snow. All possessed orenda, all were connected, even in their alienness, with her, which meant that the man who still moved toward her hut must be connected, also.

She turned her questing toward him, who was standing quietly and gazing at her empty shelter. She felt a shocking jolt as something painful and sharp met her probing thought. This was no spirit joined in the web of life that was its world, whatever world this might be. No interlinking strand bound him to the land or the sleeping vegetation. The very air seemed to avoid touching that ghastly face, which shone silver in the tenuous light.

As if her glance called to him, he turned slowly and looked into the shadows. Two-Moons stirred no muscle, though she closed her eyes to avoid having a chance glint of light on her eyeballs betray her. She felt his gaze sweep over her like a chill wind, but he did not see her, and she smiled.

One of the Onondaga would have seen her, no matter how dark the shadows or how still the one in hiding. This man did not walk the way of the forest. He had not learned the secrets of the stalker, it was plain.

However, he seemed to have other abilities to command. When he finished his survey, he straightened his cloak about his shoulders and stood straight in the middle of the patch of snow. Raising one hand, he moved it in patterns, while sparks of light, colder than firelight, brighter than fireflies, grew at the tips of his fingers.

Her eyes retained the images inscribed by those shining specks, and she could see in afterimage the shapes he was drawing. They were strange forms, which gave her a shiver down her spine and her leg bones.

He was chanting. She could barely hear his voice, so quietly did he speak. His words were alien to her ears, but something about them—the sound and the rhythm—compelled her spirit to move toward him, as he stood in the clearing. She clenched her hand upon the bone hilt of her knife until her palm and knuckles hurt. Her legs tensed, as if to rise and walk against her will. She held them quiet, but it required all her strength to do it.

Her hands strove to unclench, to push her upward and out of her hiding place.

Two-Moons-in-the-Sky recognized magic, though it was unlike any she knew. This was strong magic, though it did not draw upon any of the elements she recognized. There was no earth in it, no living plant or breathing beast; it was cold, cold, holding the feeling she sometimes knew when looking up on a cold, still night at the frozen lights winking afar in a black winter sky. This was a distant power that cared nothing for anything that lived.

Two-moons had magics of her own. In no other way could she have walked a road so different from the ways of other girls and matrons in her village.

Her mother's dreams had been true and her magics effective, yet they had not saved her from the False-Face of her vision. Knowing that, Two-Moons had fasted for days in the forest beside the lake north of her home. She had talked long with the shamans and had delved into herself with care and precision, identifying and building upon her own strengths. She had denied herself the comfort of Runs-Bucks-Down's caring, which had tempered her spirit more powerfully than any of the things that went before.

Now she relaxed, bone by bone, muscle by muscle, against the snowy ground. The bush hung about her, and the snow caught in its tangled twigs made it a secure hiding place. As if from a distance, she heard the man's voice, now shouting incomprehensible syllables into the night, as if he were angry and frustrated when she failed to emerge from hiding.

"Come forth, in the names of Orobas, of Marchocias, of Bael, I call you from hiding. In the names of Asmodeus, of Forcas, and of Buer I call you out! No shadow may hide you, no plant give you shelter. I compel you—come out!"

Two-Moons lay quietly, allowing those alien sounds to flow around and past her. Yet when he uttered those harsh names, she did feel a chill, as if an especially sharp breeze had touched her. Still, she was unmoved by his incantation. Instead, she felt an inflowing of power that told her a vision was about to appear to her. The blood slowed in her veins and her heart quieted to a steady rhythm; her hands and feet became heavy, while her eyes closed upon the snowlit scene. The warmth of Aireskoi surrounded her, and for the first time that evening she was no longer chilled to the bone.

Into her mind there crept a picture, which she studied carefully.

There was the uptilted longhouse, though in the vision it was not evening but broad day. The forest lay green on either side of the river, and there was no snow.

In the side of the house there was a doorway, and its closure, not of hide but wood, stood open, swung back against the wall of stone. As if a vital part of her were being led, she moved toward the opening and entered through it.

"This is a tower," came the soundless voice that was that of Aireskoi. "Within it lives one who possesses the power to warp the flowing of worlds and of time. He has called to you across terrible barriers for purposes that are not yours. Beware of him, for he is no friend of sun or forest or people or anything that lives. Look upon him as he labored to work his magic upon you."

The house rose like a tunnel that went up instead of sideways. Around it curled a climbing-place; though she had no material feet, Two-Moons set the shadows of hers upon the shelves of stone and moved upward, around and around as the steps followed the curve. At the end of the climb there was another doorway, and its wood closure stood open a crack. From that crack came strange smells and a light that was fire rather than sunlight.

A voice, strangely familiar, was speaking, the words crisp and firm and commanding. She recognized those names that had touched her with cold breezes as she lay beneath the bush. There were other words, as well, but she could not understand any of them. Instead, a picture within a picture formed within her mind.

There was the place where she leaned to rest her burden, the elm she knew as well as she did her own sisters. There in the midst of summer was the forest through which she had made her way in the snowstorm. That was the last spot she had truly recognized.

Just beyond it was a haze that moved like heat-shimmer between the trees. For an instant it shone distinctly, and it had the look of one of these door openings; through it she could see into a place that was no longer the familiar forest near her village. She could see that first unfamiliar oak, and past it were others, where the elm and maple wood should be.

"That is a trap he set for you, my daughter, as a child sets a snare for a rabbit. Moons ago, he created it, set to catch only one of Power, who might aid him in his wicked endeavors. Weariness and winter dulled your perceptions, or you might have felt it and avoided it, and you went through. Open this door and look into his chamber."

Two-Moons pushed lightly at the door with her indistinct hand. It swung back with a faint hiss, and the man in the room looked up from the odd things lying on a platform before him.

He turned his head, searching the chamber, but he could not see her, and she understood that she was not yet actually in his world at all. Only through the power of Aireskoi was she being shown this picture.

"The adept," Aireskoi breathed into her immaterial ear. "He is also alien to me, for he does not inhabit a world that I know or care to know. Yet because he had called upon one of mine, he has also called upon me. I understand more of him than I like to know.

"The things in those vessels have power in this task he is accomplishing. Look closely as he puts them away, for you may have need of their contents before all is done." Two-Moons watched intently as the man gazed into the vessels, which were not clay or stone as were those she knew, but were formed of some shiny stuff through which she could see their contents bubbling and steaming over a tiny point of flame. This burned beneath a metal stand, and there was another over which a pot was hissing viciously.

The adept mixed the contents of two of the containers, and the stuff turned as red as blood when it mingled. Then he added a few drops from the hissing pot. Everything turned blue, the blue of cold, of ice, of a blizzard-heavy sky.

The adept smiled, looking upon his work. Then he set

the mixture on a high shelf and covered it with something thin and flexible. Other containers on that shelf he moved into a careful order, while Two-Moons marked the places into her memory, which was trained to retain deer trails and squirrel runs and faint paths used for going to war.

Without warning, she was back inside herself, beneath that sheltering bush. The adept was moving his fingers, while sparks of blue light shot into the air and flew away into the snowy forest. Two-Moons understood, without knowing how she knew, that those sparks searched for her. Even as she had the thought, one of the sparks found her bush and settled into its snowy tangle with a hissing of steam and a strange stink.

She slipped her bow over her shoulder and tightened the string, nocking an arrow without disturbing so much as the air around her. Then she stood erect, shaking the spark down into the snow, where it guttered out.

"Why do you seek me, Burning-hand?" she asked in Iroquois.

He whirled toward her at the sound of her voice. He seemed astonished.

"You sought for me. Here I am. What is your purpose?" she asked again.

He stared at her, and she knew he did not understand her words.

She stared back, uncowed, her bow ready in her competent brown hands.

# CHAPTER TWO

## LALLIUS, THE INTRUDER

His tower chamber was stifling with the stinks and smokes rising from crucibles and retorts clamped above flames. Summer though it was, the windows of the room were tightly closed, for Lallius could not risk being detected at his work. Foresters or hunters often used the path beside the stream, and their senses were as sharp as their curiosity. He could not chance having questions raised about his presence in the tower.

Actually, he had no legal right to be there at all, or even in this convenient world lying so near the one from which he had been snatched from the headsman's axe. He was grateful that he had been able to escape to this world where necromancers and adepts were, if not accepted, at least tolerated to some extent. It had been at a terribly dangerous point in his career that Magister Albertus Parvus had summoned him here by his magical arts.

He stirred the hissing liquid in the pot, backing away slightly from the odorous steam. The mage could hardly have chosen a better time for calling a denizen of another world to this one. That sudden transition had jerked his head, quite literally, from beneath a descending axe.

That matter of his use of the corpse of a Royal Infant had not come to a good conclusion—but that was now in the distant past. He had been safe here for many years, since his rescuer brought him to this land of England, where the population was sparse and the forests thick and seemingly endless.

This tower, Albertus had told him, was the work of the greatest Master of the Age. Not one of the Master's students had dared to live here, among its secrets and spells, on a day-to-day basis. All had fled at last, leaving the new Master to find another apprentice wherever he could.

That had been Lallius, who might have no right to the tower but whose tenancy would never be disturbed. Even adepts feared the place, and the commons shunned it, avoiding even the stretch of path running along the river beside the structure.

This did not altogether please him, for where there were no commoners, there were no slaves. He had been used to having hands and feet—and lives—at his disposal, in his old life. At that time he had not determined the focus of his investigations, so curiosity and random efforts had guided his probings into the Arcana that fascinated him. Now he had a purpose, and he was focused upon a goal that compelled him toward it.

The boiling liquid foamed suddenly. He lifted the crucible with long-handled metal tongs and set it upon a bit of slate to cool. While he waited, he gnawed at an acid-stained fingernail and stared at the shelf where the esoteric books of magic were stored.

He had read them all: Michael Scott, Albertus Magnus, Arnold of Villanova, Maimonides. Their titles were worn away and their leather bindings tattered from long use and great age. It had been almost a century since he came here.

It seemed that the lives of his kind were far longer than those in this place, and he had used those years to polish his skills to a very high level. Far beyond, he mused, the abilities of Albertus Parvus, his rescuer.

The stuff in the crucible was cooling, though its purplish surface still roiled with bubbles. He lifted another vessel from his work table and measured a few drops into the crucible. Then he poured the mixture into a glass beaker, where it turned the color of fresh blood.

Even his cold and ancient heart beat quickly as he knew the time had come at last. The potion was ready, the lessons of the masters well learned. It was time to set his trap in that other part of this world, where he had detected the presence of primitive people.

They seemed to be hunter-gatherers, with the rudiments of agriculture already established. They would be defenseless against his powers, and would make excellent slaves, for to have advanced to that point they could not be stupid.

He took the potion up and moved carefully toward the long, stained settle along the wall behind his rank of equipment. There he sat down cautiously, leaned back so as not to fall, and upended the beaker. He downed its contents in one gulp, closed his eyes at the terrible taste, and swung his feet onto the settle. Lying flat, he forced himself to relax against the disturbance the stuff caused in his stomach.

Using his far-seeing methods, he had watched a certain spot in the forest where those primitives lived. There was a path from the village through the forest to a lake where the people hunted and fished. It was perfect for his purposes. In his mind he formed a doorway between that spot and the forest downriver from the tower. He had done this many times that summer, and he would do it many more, using different ingredients and different techniques. One day, he knew he would succeed in setting his trap.

* * * * * * *

The summer had seemed long, and now snow covered the forest and the path that held his doorway. The stream was iced over, so that if anyone came, he could approach the tower easily. Lallius grew fidgety when no one came, even the locals who sometimes ventured as far as the river bend some half mile from the black tower. Waiting was not a thing he did with any grace.

He reread the books, though he had memorized them decades before, even those in unfamiliar languages that he had been forced to learn before understanding them. He paced through the tower, every chamber, every stairway, even the moldy depths beneath it and the breathless platform on the roof. As he waited for his trap to spring, he found that nothing seemed to calm his mind.

By midwinter his nerves seemed like harp strings, strung to the snapping point. But he knew the time was upon him. One morning he woke with the conviction that now was the time. That night he felt as if something twanged sharply inside him, as if an invisible tripwire had been triggered. His game was in the snare, he knew without doubt.

The shaman (he had no doubt it would be a man with the modest powers one might expect of a primitive) would come to his door, for he had set a compulsion upon the path, the stream, even the forest itself. That had been difficult, for this forest knew him to be alien, and it had been resistant to his spells.

Pacing round and round his cluttered room, he continued to wait, but heard no sound from downstream. Surely any approaching step would crunch in the snow!

At last he could no longer bear the cold darkness, and struck flint to steel in order to kindle a lamp. Its ruddy light threw a path from his high window across a long expanse of snow. He stared out, seeing nothing in the track of the light. Beyond that, the darkness seemed impenetrable.

He knew his prey was coming—he could feel it along invisible webs of sensing. Surely the trapped one must obey his compulsions and had come upstream instead of going down. Lallius sank again onto the settle and tried to compose his mind.

His masters in that old world had warned him. Only those who control their own powers and reactions to power could be expected to command the effects of their spells and incantations. If he lost control now, he might well lose all he had worked so hard to achieve.

He closed his eyes against the glare of the lamp and concentrated upon relaxing. He must have succeeded, for some time later he jerked into wakefulness and sat upright. Some sound troubled the night—distant, strange—he listened intently and nodded.

A voice was singing a chant. He could make out a word now and then, but it was gibberish. Still, that would not have waked him in itself. The flow of Power had given him the twinge that hooked him out of sleep.

Someone below in the forest was calling upon a power he did not recognize. He rose and went to the window, and he felt upon his skin the direction from which the song came. Lallius went into his sleeping chamber to find his heavy cloak, taking with him no light.

He moved as surely as a cat in darkness, and so he left the tower and moved onto the snowy ice. Once he reached the bank of the stream, he looked about, using his night vision to survey the area.

There was a faint track leading into the wood. There was a glade there, and he felt the source of the song as coming from that spot. He moved toward it, careless of the noise made by his feet.

In the glade was a tiny hut made of branches, sprouted like some alien fungus since the day before. This must be where his prey hid—yet how could that shaman or native sorcerer elude the spell? It should have brought him directly to the tower.

Lallius approached the hut, all his senses alert. Before he arrived, he knew that it was empty, though the aura of life still hung about it. Seconds ago, its tenant had left and must be very near, even now.

The adept stood beside the small heap of branches and stared into the shadows, turning to sweep the entire area. There seemed to be only white snow and black shadow. Nothing showed a suspicious shape or motion.

Thanks to his powers, he was not limited to sight alone. Lallius lifted his hands and drew the Arcana upon the air. Sparks of energy flared at his fingertips, and even he could feel the tension of the drawing-spell as it formed around him. His victim must feel it, too, his muscles moving to the will of another. That would be a terrifying thing to one who had never before encountered it.

Something struggled, tugging at the net of his concentration. He smiled with satisfaction—and then it was gone as if it had never been. Surely his quarry could not have escaped! No, this must be a more potent captive than he had dreamed of acquiring. He lay in the shadows, very near, and he had powers of his own, primitive without doubt, and yet with a certain amount of potency. They would be ineffective, ultimately, against his own long years of discipline and study, Lallius knew, and yet his frustration grew. This must end.

He drew a deep breath and intoned those names of Power that could force the hidden one to come forth. No one came. Nothing moved. There was no feeling of resistance—there was simply nothing to receive the summons.

Sweat beaded on his forehead, even though the night was very cold. Lallius had not dreamed that there could be anyone of any kind who might ignore those potent names. In his own dimension they were as powerful as they seemed in this one. Surely they must rule over all the inhabitants of this planet!

Lallius moved his fingers, his will set upon forcing the hidden one out. He spun off blue sparks of energy designed to seek out life of whatever kind. Those went whirling into the trees, hissing occasionally against snow-covered branches.

He turned, watching them as they ranged across the night. One moved directly toward a clump of bushes beside the river and caught amid its icy twigs. He wondered if this might be chance, or if someone actually hid there.

There came a slight quiver in the bush and a robed shape rose easily to its feet to face him. Standing erect, it held a weapon he had seen others in this world use. A crude bow was strung, and an arrow was set to the string.

Before he could move, the person spoke a string of meaningless syllables. The voice left him stunned, for it was that of a woman. The challenge of that shape and its stance had assured him this had to be a male. What had he caught in that trap in the forest, halfway across time and this world?

She moved toward him, and he knew he had not commanded that. Now she was out of the shadow, and he could see her robe was made of finely dressed hide. Her hair was very long, as black as the night, bound tightly into a thick tail at the crown of her head. Her eyes were dark wells in a face that seemed only a slightly paler shadow in the snow light. He felt in their unseen depths a cold assessment that made even him shiver.

He had made a spell to catch one of power, untaught, a primitive savage just setting his feet upon the ladder of learning. Could those distant, dark-skinned people be more than they had appeared to be to his watching eyes?

As if reading his mind, the woman laughed. Then she spoke, but again he did not understand her words. But a gesture informed him that she intended to spend the night in his tower. He was surprised. She did not have him at her mercy, arrow or no arrow. Once she was in the tower she would be at his mercy, though that was not a thing he had ever possessed.

# CHAPTER THREE

## The Visions of Runs-Bucks-Down

Even through the smoke and noise of the crowded longhouse, Runs-Bucks-Down could feel the empty spot where Two-Moons should be, in her space at the end of the house. Her sisters Laughs-Too-Much and Deer-Eyes could not fill the gap she left when she did not return on time from one of her expeditions.

He was watching the door flap every time the deer hide swung to admit another person who lived with this clan. It was unbecoming to a man and a warrior to worry so much about a woman who was not his wife, so he pretended to concentrate on chipping a perfect edge on a spear or arrow tip or checking his shafts for straightness. As he worked and watched, he tried to keep his face properly impassive, but he found it very hard to do.

Tonight his heart was not at ease. Snow fell outside, and the wind whistled past the curves of the longhouse. She had been gone too long. Though Two-Moons had rejected his offer and turned him away from her place in the lodge, he knew it was not through lack of caring. She had made that very clear to him, and he understood, for he was another who dreamed true.

That did not ease his pain, for he knew she was not destined to be a wife. She was suited to be a warrior and a

Dreamer, though that had been a hard thing to accept.

Her refusal should have removed her from his concerns, but it had not. Something within him knew when she came and when she went, and now that something stirred impatiently inside, insisting that things were not well with Two-Moons-in-the-Sky. He felt no spark of warmth where he sensed her life, even when she was away from the longhouse.

From the corner of his eye he saw a hand push aside the deerskin closing off her living space. A large dark eye peered forth, looking toward the doorway, before the hide slipped back into place. By its continued motion, he knew the girl's hand still clutched it, for the sisters were waiting and had begun to worry. Their sister might be skillful and brave, but she was not large, and her strength was not that of a man.

He knew as well as they that there were always dangers. A bear roused from winter dreams, a branch loosened by the wind in the forest, a wounded buck, horns gory with her blood—the thoughts were intolerable. He had to know, whether or not it was beneath his dignity.

There was, however, no need to let the entire clan know what he was about to do. He folded his arrows neatly into their hide pouch and secured it to his shoulder. He wrapped his heavy fur blanket about his shoulder to hide the fact that he had his weapons with him. Then, as if to stretch his legs, he stood, shrugged, and made his way toward the door-hide.

He could feel Laughs staring at his back as he stepped outside and let the hides drop into place behind him. The wind was terribly cold, and the snow was falling even faster than before. He was glad of the bearskin blanket, for it would be a bad night to be out without such protection.

By now he was sure that Two-Moons would be camped safely in some sheltered spot in the forest, if she had gone too far to make it back to the longhouse that night. Yet he had no secure feeling that this was what she had done. Something nagged at him, pulling him away from the cluster of longhouses that made up the village, out of the stockade and across its circling moat.

He had worn his double-thick moccasins, knowing that he would need that protection, and now he set them upon the trail toward the lake. That was the direction Two-Moons had taken when she left that morning. Unless she had made a great circle, she must return the same way.

He followed the game trail, his feet finding its texture without effort. Past the elms and maples he went, feeling his way as much by the talents that made him a Dreamer as by sight. That was as well, for the snow was now so thick that it was impossible to see. Even breathing was difficult, for the blowing flakes tried to clog his nostrils.

No track could have been left on the trail, with the blizzard blowing so hard. Even his own tracks were obliterated almost before he passed. When he came to the biggest elm he paused, setting one hand against the cold ridges of its bark.

Something tingled from the bark to his hand, moving into his flesh from the tree. He straightened and stood motionless for several heartbeats, huddled into his bearskin and thinking hard.

So close to the longhouse, it seemed strange to build a brush hut and sit there in the snow, waiting for a vision, yet this was the thing all his instincts told him to do. Thankfully, he had fasted that day and was prepared.

He bundled leafy branches and tied them down over springy bushes to make a tiny shelter. Snow banked around its edges kept out the worst of the wind, and he even pushed it into a barrier before the entry-hole. Then, enveloped in his bearskin except for his face, he crawled into the hut and sat cross-legged, protecting his body in the folds of fur. He must wait, for visions did not come just for the wishing. He had prepared as well as he could, and now he waited upon the spirits that lived in all things, linked by orenda. He waited also upon the Master of Life, Aireskoi, who sometimes came to the aid of his children. From scalp lock to fingers to toes he relaxed, upright, eyes closed. The elm, against which he had set one side of his shelter, was silent in the snow, yet he seemed to hear a whisper from its leafless branches. Something was trying to communicate with him, but he would not pry into the tree's secrets. Patient as stone, he waited for the tree to remember what had happened that evening.

Linked to the tree through their common orenda, he allowed himself to sink into its being. He felt the buffeting of the wind, the sap-snapping chill of the night. He felt, for a short moment, the living warmth of Two-Moons' shoulder as she rested against the trunk. Then she was gone from the elm, and he reached out toward other growing things that might hold in their cells the memory of her passing. There were trees that had felt the brush of her cloak or of the deer carcass, the warmth of her breath on the air. Bushes had bent and returned to position as she passed. And then there was a great blank space, which held no trace of her at all.

Runs-Bucks breathed deeply, reaching into the frozen grasses beneath the snow. No recent pressure except his own passage was recorded in their stems. He reached deeper still, to the tiny mosses below. A slight weight had borne upon them, though the memory was almost gone. He moved along those tiny linkages to a spot beyond which there was no memory of any foot.

He opened his eyes and stared into the darkness. He had followed the path to this point. She had not veered from it and had been upon it when the last trace was left behind her. Yet where could she be?

She was not on the path, though she had been recently enough to show she was returning home. She was not in the longhouse. Only a True Vision, very rare and never to be invited lightly, could reveal to him her whereabouts. To ask for such a vision, he should be surrounded by all the shamans of the clans and perhaps even those from other villages. Yet it would be wrong, he felt in his deepest instinct, to move from this spot and lose the tenuous link he had found.

He sat even straighter and breathed a deep breath of freezing air. "Maker of Life, I sit here waiting. I have done all I can do and have not found Two-Moons-in-the-Sky. She is not where all my sensing tells me she should be. Only You, who formed all that is, who breathes life into man and flower and fish and animal and all things that live, can find her.

"Here she rested, just before she vanished. She carried a deer, for the elm felt its pelt against the bark and the dying warmth of its body. Master of Life, I await a Vision."

Straight-backed, cross-legged, he waited, wrapped in his bearskin, in the little shelter. The snow died at last to a light riffle, the wind to a whisper. Night marched across the sky, and at last dawn edged up the eastern sky, paling it to silver. Snow and wind died away together, leaving the wood stark white and deep black, sketched in webbed lines of branch and root and bole. Runs-Bucks-Down felt the coming of dawn, though he did not open his eyes, but he did not pay heed. Here he must wait until he was given a sign to guide him. When the first of the women came down the path to find wood for their fires, he did not answer their questions or note their going. The sun struck the frozen world with eye-piercing brightness. An elder of his clan came up the path to squat beside his hut. This was the truest of the Dreamers, far too wise to trouble a seeker with questions or comments. Instead, he cocked his grizzled head, closed his black eyes, and opened his own orenda to that of the younger man.

What he read there brought him upright in one jerky motion. He stood beside the crude shelter and set his own eyes, heart, and spirit to aid Runs-Bucks-Down.

The day passed. Children ran out into the snow to gather kindling-wood from deadfall in the forest, to call and chant and sing and jump. Women walked around the two men who blocked their trail, making ill-tempered comments at times, though neither Dreamer noticed them.

Night fell again, and no one lingered in the wood except the pair beside the elm. And at last the Vision came, one that neither the old nor the young Dreamer found himself able to decipher.

As Runs-Bucks sat in this even colder night, sweat began to pour from his skin. Something strange, frightening, formed before him, freezing his limbs into immobility, locking his mind into astonishment. As the vision unfolded, he became aware that Okton-iyo, he of the Beautiful Spirit, had joined him, standing beside his shelter. That knowledge gave him the strength to look again upon the thing he must see.

Between the trees, which now were only dark bulks and lines against the new snow, a pale shimmer was forming, opening into a place he could neither recognize nor explain. Beyond it bulked the shapes of huge trees, gnarled and thick-branched, not slender like the maples and elms. He was, he realized, seeing into a world that was not the one he knew. He could see a stream there, its icy span almost covered with snow. He could hear the gurgle of water flowing beneath the ice, and beside it was a path, upon whose stretch of white were shadows, the marks of small moccasins. Shockingly, the Vision broke apart, leaving him numb and bewildered. A hand touched him, pulled him back into his body. Beautiful Spirit had reached into his hut and touched his shoulder, shaking him roughly. Roused now, he crawled out and stood beside the old man.

"What did we see?" he asked Okton-iyo. "Where was it? Two-Moons has gone there, for my spirit knows it, but where is there? How can I help her?"

The old man grunted. "Taonhiawagi has granted us both a Vision, son of my brother. I had never thought to have such a gift, and now it must be considered by all the Dreamers. The shamans of the Clan-Houses must think on this.

"Our sister-warrior has gone through a doorway, and not by her own will. Some terrible shaman has called her spirit to him, and her body went as well. Let us go back to the longhouse, for there is much to consider here."

# CHAPTER FOUR

## Two-Moons in the Tower

The white-faced man moved ahead of Two-Moons, crossing the ice-locked stream and moving toward the tall house. He walked arrogantly, his head high, but Two-Moons knew he was not as certain of her as he tried to seem. She could see a betraying quiver in his shoulders; walking slightly behind, she could see the tense muscles in his cheek and jaw. Even in the snow light and half hidden by the hood, she could tell he was as tense as a bow-string.

She did not speak but walked behind, bow half drawn, as he approached the door-slab of that strangest of houses. The wooden part swung backward, and as he moved forward she followed so closely she stepped upon his heel. He might well turn quickly, once inside, and try to catch her off-guard. Indeed, he half turned, but she prodded him with the tip of her arrow, hard enough to make him wince. He moved toward the steps she had climbed in her vision, and she knew that to be a difficult place to use a bow. She relaxed it and slipped her knife into her belt, ready to hand. However, she no longer considered it necessary to continue as captor and captive. In this alien world, there was no place to which she might flee.

Besides, one did not trap a person against whom one held no reason for vengeance. If he had taken so much trouble, it was unlikely he meant her harm.

34

She said, "Stop!"

Hearing her voice, he paused, one foot raised to the first step. Turning, he looked directly into her eyes. By the light that came down the shaft from the well lit room above, she could see that his eyes were weird, pale as a stormy sky, cold as the frozen river. They were frankly studying her.

"Peace," she said in her Onondaga tongue. "Kayaner-enh!" He frowned, uncomprehending. She made signs with her hands, first slinging her bow behind her shoulder. "It is not necessary to continue as enemies, unless you insist upon that. We are here. Where might I go?

"You have brought me from my own home for some purpose, it is clear. Perhaps I may help you with that and return to my own place. Until we can speak together to learn that, why should be not have peace between us?"

No sign of understanding lit that slab-like face, but he did not try to attack her, even though the bow was slung and the knife invisible beneath her cloak. Instead, he turned and climbed rapidly to a door—not the one through which she had looked when Aireskoi guided her spirit there. He opened the wood and stepped back to allow her to enter the space beyond it.

She stepped into something altogether outside of her experience. A rounded room, one side flat against the stair landing, was filled with things, whose uses she could guess at, although she had never seen anything like them. There was a flat platform, obviously for sleeping, though it held no comfortable pile of furs. Another platform, like the one she had envisioned in his workroom, stood on legs in the middle of the room, with sitting-places around it.

Most interesting were the dark leather oblongs stacked on shelves around the walls. One lay on the table, folded back upon itself to show pale leaf-like sheets, which were covered with marks. It reminded her of clan records kept by the shaman, who drew pictures of important events in charcoal on birch bark.

A fire burned in a cave in the farther wall. The smoke seemed to be pulled upward without fogging the room, which spoke well of the intelligence of those who built this shelter. She slipped her cloak from her shoulders and moved toward it, kneeling to warm her frozen hands.

The stranger made no move as he watched her, his pale face ruddied by firelight, which made it seem more human and less deathlike. He looked puzzled, his face showing his emotions, unlike the habit of her own people. His lips pressed together tightly, as if he were displeased.

Why should he be? She had not harmed him, yet, even though she could have skewered him on her arrow many times over.

Standing, she moved back to shrug her cloak about her shoulders. "What a shame it is that we cannot speak together," she said to him. "How, otherwise, may I learn why you brought me here and what your purposes may be? How did you learn of my people? How did you learn of me? I think it may be that only through you will I be able to return to my home, but without talking that may not be possible."

She felt a deep sadness, and it made her ashamed. A warrior of the Onondaga did not allow his emotions to come forth so clearly, even if he were enduring the Honorable Death. For the first time she wondered if that might be a reason for the trap she had stumbled into. Had this one entrapped her to give her the honor of torture and death in the manner of her own kind?

There was no war between them, she was certain. They did not even inhabit the same world. Even when she came into his place, she had not spied upon him in flesh but had gone to her own shelter and remained there. She was sure that Aireskoi had shielded her spirit from him, and he had not known she was present in his chamber while he worked.

But who knew what alien customs others might have? There was no sign of any women here, and they were the ones who devised the most painful and terrible tests of courage. There was no suitable fire, no stake arranged for such a ceremony. No elders had gathered to witness the test and do honor to the guest, to feed and talk with her during lulls in the activities.

Indeed, as she looked into his colorless eyes and pinched face, she felt that this one would not understand that torture was a thing of mutual courtesy and esteem, honoring both hosts and guest. She would not, she realized, want to learn about any custom of this colorless kind. His habits would not be concerned with honor, her deepest instinct told her.

She allowed nothing to show on her face as she thought. Instead she looked closely at the room, seeking for any other opening than the one behind her. A square hole, something less than the width of her shoulders, marked the wall before her, stopped with another of the wooden panels. There were fastenings inside it, keeping it closed against the cold wind outside. It was not designed for keeping a prisoner within. She did not allow her gaze to linger there but looked again at the table, noting that it held flat containers of food. She bent over it and touched the flat bit—a kind of bread, she thought. Meat was there, cooked with some herb that lent its tang.

A knife lay beside it, not made of flint but of some strange shining stuff. That interested her. She touched the bright stuff of the blade and a line of blood followed that touch. Very sharp!

The man came forward now, speaking again. Though she did not know his words, she listened to their sounds: "Eat what you will. I will leave you to rest. I wonder about you—if you were not one of power, the trap would not have sprung, yet a woman—a primitive.... I must think about this. I must look again into the books, but I am sure there is nothing there about such as you. If you were a demon...."

Muttering, he took up the knife to cut a thick slab of the dark bread, another chunk of meat, and laid them upon a wooden tray. While nothing more was said, his gestures told her to eat, then to sleep. That was good, for at this point she had no idea what else she might find to do.

The door closed behind him, leaving her to take bread into her hands and return to the fire. There she sat on the floor, staring into the blaze and trying to create some logical pattern from the strange series of events since she went hunting the day before.

None of her people had ever spoken of anything like this, though many had seen the dreaded False-Face in the forest. Now she wondered if this strange man might have looked into her homeland and been seen by those with some power of perception. If he could set a trap there, she felt he might well be able to do more.

The bread was strange but acceptable. The meat was overcooked, but she ate it ravenously, her energies depleted by cold and stress.

Although the fire burned without filling the room with smoke, she could tell, sitting so close, that much of the heat went up the hole that carried away the smoke. But at least that wind did not enter the chamber except in thin gusts that seeped in around the opening in the wall.

At last she wiped her fingers on her buckskin leggings and unstrung her bow. She set it beside the sleeping place, with the arrows arranged neatly beside it, ready to hand. The man had carried away that bright knife with which he cut the bread and meat, but her own strong knife of flint was like a part of her hand. She set it beside her hip as she lay down and covered herself with her outer robe.

The fire was dying away to coals, but the deep ashes and the chunk of wood she had laid on it should hold sparks that would let her kindle it anew in the morning.

Now she straightened her weary bones and closed her eyes.

Before she was completely relaxed she heard a soft sound outside the door. Something slid quietly, and there came a soft bump and a click. Two-Moons sat and stood in one fluid motion. Her moccasined feet moved silently on the floor as she approached the door. She touched the latch as she had seen the man do when he left. The thing moved up and down, but when she pushed against the door it was held fast.

In some manner, she had been fastened into the room. Suddenly she was no longer weary or cold or ill-at-ease. Never had she been confined against her will, and this was not something she could or would endure.

The last of the fire logs broke half from half, and now the fire was only red coals. By their light, she reassembled her weapons and tied on her cloak. She once again donned her second set of moccasins, now dry from the fire, and prepared to face the weather outside.

The window fastenings were strange to her, but they were simple enough, and she soon had them loose and the wooden closure swung outward with a hiss of metal on metal. She froze, listening, for any of her own kind would have heard and would be up, investigating such a sound in their own home at night. But there was no sign the pale-faced man had heard, wherever he might be for the night.

She leaned out and looked down. Below, the shaft of the tower went down very far—farther than she had looked down from the top of the tallest tree she had climbed as a child. The black stone of its wall was banded in layers, and the weather had eaten away cracks where the courses came together.

The snow light was almost too bright, now that the wind had died down and snowflakes no longer blurred the air. Pale reflections allowed her to see where a foot or a hand might find purchase. Without hesitation, Two-Moons stepped over the edge of the window and slid a foot down onto the first ridge. Then, foot by hand by foot, she made her way down the sheer face of the building, as she was used to making her way up and down and along cliffs and steeps of the Mountain that was the pride of the Onondaga.

The last of the ridges was two man-heights above the ground, but she had leaped much farther than this, just for the sport of it. Dropping her bow and arrows, she marked the place where they fell. Then she launched herself outward, into the snow bank beside the river.

She landed with a muffled thump, gathered up her possessions, and headed once more for the tiny shelter she had built when she first arrived here. She might go into the tower of her own will, but that man must understand that he could not imprison an Onondaga Dream-Maker.

She had food there. She had her warm cloak-robe and her fur undergarments. She had already constructed her hut. One of her kind needed no more to survive a night in the snow, however cold the wind might blow.

Once she settled herself cross-legged in the shelter, wrapped the robe about her entire body, and found her own warm center of certainty, she slept at once. The will can force the body to great efforts, but once the need is past a wise man rests.

Tomorrow might hold even greater demands.

# CHAPTER FIVE

## LALLIUS RECONSIDERS

The adept did not sleep deeply. He was filled with bewilderment, excitement, and apprehension in equal measures. On the previous night he had been completely confused by the strangeness of his catch. The lack of communication was a problem—gestures lacked enough meanings and flexibility to achieve understanding.

Morning brought more balance to his mind. In the frosty chill of dawn he breakfasted, then he was ready to face this unexpected quarry who was to be his tool—perhaps even his ally—with suitable dignity and display of power.

The bolt was still shot as he approached her door. There was no sign that she had tried to force it, and it was possible that a people so primitive had no concept of locks. Civilization created thievery, he knew too well, though there had been wise men in his own world who had not wanted to believe that.

He slipped back the rod and opened the door.

A faint spark still lit the hearth where the last lingering coals were dying. The bed was empty, but the window swung wide, letting in the cold gray dawn. She was not in the room. The bucket he had placed there for the convenience of his captive was empty, and most of the food had not been touched.

He moved to stare down from the window; thirty feet of sheer stone dropped straight down to the rocky ground of the island. Could this alien woman fly then? The thought made him shudder.

Then he saw the dark depression in the snow bank off to the left and a line of smaller dots marking the snow toward the river. She had climbed down the tower in the darkness and leaped almost twice her height to land in the snow. Those tracks led purposefully toward the glade where her rude shelter had been built the night before.

Lallius retreated into the chamber and closed the shutter, fastening it with unsteady fingers. She would be, he knew, sitting in that small hut. She had not been escaping from him—if that had been true, those prints would have led anywhere except the spot where he had found her.

No, she had informed him, as plainly as words would have done, that she would not be imprisoned. She would not be compelled. She would only stay in his tower upon her own terms.

Lallius had never encountered such an attitude, either in his own place, where one must be a tyrant or a sycophant, or here. In this society, what he had seen of it as he journeyed with Master Albertus, it had been much the same. The books left for him in the tower had not contradicted that notion.

Did this woman rule in her own land? That seemed unlikely, though in his own place there had, from time to time, been supremely strong and cruel women who had achieved such power. But a ruler would not have been wandering in the night, burdened with the dead animal he had seen in the hut. Was she one of power? He could not tell, although her actions the night before hinted at it.

She was just too alien for him to decide.

He wished suddenly and devoutly that Master Albertus had survived to advise him. The adept had swept him across the dimensions, saving his neck from the axe, and had then shared with him his great knowledge. Master Albertus had been a pupil of the Great One, Albertus Magnus, whose powers had been different from those Lallius knew, alien in their potency.

The wizard had spent almost a half century poring over the tomes the Masters had left in this tower, and he knew that twice that time would not have given him enough knowledge and skill to match Albertus Parvus, much less his mentor. How had such short-lived men acquired so much in their brief lifetimes? Albertus had died too soon, and he could not return.

Lallius sighed, turned on his heel, and went into his study. There piles of moldering books filled the shelves and were stacked on the floor in untidy heaps. Surely there must be some mention there, if anyone before him had ever drawn into this dimension someone like that dark-skinned woman with steady black eyes.

He must seek until he found something to guide him before he took his next step. He must act without error, if he was to achieve his purpose.

A sudden thought stopped him in his tracks. If she were typical of her kind, how might he enslave them, even if he pulled through between the dimensions enough of them to serve his needs?

He dropped into his rump-sprung chair and leaned his head on one long, acid-stained hand. Slaves must, by their nature, be docile, subservient, relatively helpless against unknown abilities. They must be open to instruction and discipline. It was quite clear that this woman was not made of such material.

Yet to change his plan at this point meant that his long years of study and preparation must begin all over again, centered upon another place on this world and another time-span. He must spend more months of drinking stinking potions and concentrating upon distant places, conjuring up another doorway for yet another kind of prey. And was there any promise that such prey would be more suitable than this?

Lallius straightened his back, set his feet on the floor, and leaned forward to open a thick book, from which green mildew puffed away in an acrid cloud.

"She has Power," he said to the page of crabbed Latin. "Therefore, she is not typical of her people. Possibly she may not even be typical of their priests. I may have succeeded in finding someone who is at odds with her own kind, which would be fortunate. She might have no scruples about helping me to trap and enslave them, even if she could understand my purposes and my methods.

"Perhaps the Dark Lord has his eye upon me, after all these years of effort. Perhaps I have succeeded better than I know."

He ran a skinny finger down the page, moving his lips as he deciphered the antique script. Yet he found no help there; he frowned and flung the book onto the cluttered floor. Another fared no better. Soon he sat amid a litter of discarded books and parchments, scrolls and letters. In none of the literature could he find any description matching that of his captured woman.

Demons abounded. People from his own dimension were described in recognizable detail. Shaggy half-beasts from some shuddery past had come through doorways set too carelessly in insufficiently explored places. There was no description that in any way matched this capture.

Again he leaned on his hand, his eyes half closed. It was vital that he find someone to share his knowledge, to teach his power. He must have companions, for even for his long-lived kind he was growing old. He was lonely, and his work suffered for lack of another mind against which to hone his thoughts.

Yet he could never leave this tower and explore the England to which Albertus had brought him. He knew nothing of their present laws and manners, for he had been absent from that briefly seen world for a century. He would betray himself, sooner or later, and then he would face another disaster like that which had placed his head beneath the axe. Oh, Lallius had seen the countryside as they traveled, for Albertus had not hidden him. He had taken pains to show his guest the high points of his country as they drove past them in the rattling and jouncing carriage. He had even bribed dungeon-keepers to allow them to observe a questioning in Paris, in which an old woman had been torn apart, bit by bit, during the interrogation.

When asked, the jailor told them she was thought to have some knowledge of a crime committed by her neighbor, who could not be found for questioning. Lallius, knowing that he had surely deserved the fate he escaped in his other life, had shuddered, for this seemed barbarism of the worst sort. However, he said nothing of that to Albertus, who seemed proud of the ingenuity of the torturers.

It had been worse in London. Feeling safe amid the great crowd gathered for the occasion, Albertus took him to watch a hanging, drawing, and quartering of one who had opposed the policies of the king. That was not a civilized spectacle. Beside it, the work of the headsman seemed a marvel of mercy and quickness.

When he had been much younger and less informed about other ways, Lallius had thought the laws and punishments of his own country to be inhumane. After seeing the workings of this world, which considered itself enlightened and advanced, he decided never to expose himself to any risk of suffering a punishment like those he had seen.

The risks he had taken in his own place now made him shiver to think of the risk he might take here. He had heard tales of the punishment of witches in their travels, and by definition, he was such a one. Nothing as gentle as a swift death beneath an axe might be expected here.

With a sigh, he sat once more. The tiny fire was almost out in the grate, and he dropped to his knees and blew upon the coals as he added tinder. When the fire blazed again, he sat back on his heels and looked into the flames.

"If I cannot compel her, perhaps I can persuade her," he said aloud. "And in order to persuade her, I must teach her a common language. My own? Or the Italian of the Master? Or this illogical English?

"She might pass for an Italian, perhaps, if she were bathed and dressed properly. What is best to do? Ah, Master Albertus, I would that you were here with me. This is a riddle that two might read more easily than one."

# CHAPTER SIX

## COUNCIL IN THE CLAN HOUSE

Runs-Bucks-Down was exhausted, and he knew that Okton-iyo must be as well. Though the old man had endured fewer frozen hours of vigil than he, still he had been standing all the while. For a day and most of a night the elder had shared the watch in the forest.

Runs-Bucks looked down at the old man as they neared the clan house. "We will see with clearer eyes if we sleep now and call the shamans and the Dreamers tomorrow," he said. "Do you not agree?"

"It is so," the old Dreamer replied. "I am not so young as I once was, and my bones feel worn away to the very marrow. Let us sleep the hours of darkness and talk when the sun is high again."

Even lying in his furs among his kin, Runs-Bucks found it hard to rest, for the vision of that strange opening in the forest hung behind his eyelids. Those footprints in the snowy path burned in his mind, leading away and stopping suddenly and completely. He ached to run after their maker, following until he found Two-Moons and learned where she had gone, but he remained still and calm on his pallet.

Beyond him, his mother and his father breathed deeply. His young sister laughed in her sleep. At last he slept, to the music of their breathing.

It was not difficult to bring together all the wise folk of the village, deep in the winter. The fall hunting and fishing were done, the crops harvested, the wild nuts and seeds and fruits secured for winter use. Now clans remained cooped together in their longhouses, and it was a time of tale-telling at best, boredom and quarrels at worst. Something new to occupy minds was welcome, however grim the circumstances might be. The elders, the shamans, the Dreamers, and the families joined together in the middle of the longhouse to hear the tale told by Runs-Bucks-Down and Okton-iyo. Only the children were sent outside to play in the snow, so their noise and games would not disturb their elders.

Because he was the older Dreamer, it was fitting that Okton-iyo tell the tale of the Vision sent to them both by the Master of Life. This he did with quiet force, and when he was done, the other elders questioned him closely.

"The dreadful False Face appears just so to those who walk in the forest," Odatsehe, chief of the elders, said. "I have heard from the lips of those who were ill or dying that fearful countenances, warped and evil, formed in the midst of the air, and they were bodiless. Are you certain that, weary and fasting as you both were, this is not what you saw?"

Okton-iyo smiled without resentment. "At the very time of the vision, I watched intently, thinking that I might be led into error by my weariness and the cold. But no, it was no False-Face we saw. This was nothing that any of our people has ever spoken about seeing. Or, if they should have seen it, they have not returned to tell of it.

"Only one of our kind has passed through that strangeness, and that was Two-Moons-in-the-Sky, for the grasses and the bushes and the trees spoke of her presence, up to that point. And then she was gone, and beyond that place of the vision there was nothing to indicate she had been there. She is not here, where she should be if she had been able to come."

Odatsehe's face was expressionless as he nodded. Behind him his mother, Iyo-Wakonnyh, stared fixedly at his back. Although the old woman did not like or approve of the life Two-Moons had chosen, she was, nevertheless, a woman of the Tortoise Clan, a kinswoman, and a Dreamer of great power. She was gravely concerned, and Runs-Bucks felt sure that her son could feel her gaze against his back.

Runs-Bucks said nothing and showed less, but his heart felt lighter to know that the Matron of the clan supported the cause of Two-Moons. Even as he thought, Odatsehe turned to look into his eyes.

The young warrior sat cross-legged before the fire and began to tell the long tale once more. Although it did not enhance his dignity to admit such concern for a woman who was not his wife, he spoke with feeling. The woman was, after all, a warrior and a "brother," and that erased any stigma he might have suffered because of his intensity.

Now he leaned forward. "And so at last Taonhiawagi sent a vision to me and to Okton-iyo, as he has described to you. It is not a vision easy to read, though we now know our brother traveled that way to another place that is not in our forest. We must follow, but how may that be done?

"There is no mark upon the path to reveal that doorway again, though we walked forward and back, seeking it. Some powerful shaman has called her, I feel it in my heart. What can we, her brothers, do to bring her back to us?" He looked slowly around the circle, took the pipe that was passed to him, and puffed upon it twice.

Odatsehe stared into the fire, and the Dreamers did the same. This required much thought, perhaps even true Dreams, and now the others, warriors and women alike, rose to go about their daily tasks. Only those who were

Dreamers and leaders of the clan remained seated about the council fire. The day seemed to move with painful slowness as they considered how to guide their people. A decision might well affect the destiny of the entire village and all its clans. Not one uttered ill-thought speculations. No light suggestion passed their lips, for that was not the way of the Onondaga. Only after the most intense consideration would one of these people offer his or her thought upon the subject.

As the day waned, Runs-Bucks began to believe they would come to no conclusion, suggest no course of action. The fires were kindled in the families' places, where women prepared food for the smallest children. Most of the clan went to their rest, yet the circle still sat about the fire that the Matron had mended before going to her own bed.

They sat so still it seemed they did not even breathe. The wind had died outside, and only the sputter of the fire interrupted the faint sounds of the sleepers about them.

At last Kowa-okonha, Great-Son, the youngest of the Dreamers, raised his head and gazed around the circle. "This is too large a problem for one clan to solve. There would be no shame in calling our fellows for aid as we think about this. I am too young among you to know what is best to be done. I feel the need of help."

A long breath that was almost a sigh—too controlled to be quite that—rose from the circle. Each of those about the fire had evidently been thinking the same thing for some time. Each obviously felt his pride would be lessened if the suggestion came from his lips, but the youngest of them all could not be dishonored for making the suggestion. He was a beginner, and modest, and now he had their gratitude.

Odatsehe rose stiffly and stretched his back before turning toward his bed-place. "Tomorrow," he said, "we will call upon the other clans. Together, surely, we will find a way to aid Two-Moons-in-the-Sky. Now we must rest."

Once more, Runs-Bucks lay still on the shelf with his family, controlling his impatience with difficulty. An entire day had passed, and nothing had been decided. Impatience was an enemy he had been taught to control in order to attain the fullness of wisdom, but now he ached to go out into the night in order to wrest some further sign from the spirits or the Master of Life.

However, he knew he had already been given a sign that required the aid of his fellows. Now he and they must make the best possible use of it, so he sighed, one long silent breath, and closed his eyes. He kept them closed resolutely, and after a while he slept. His dreams were not happy ones.

Morning found a full gathering of Dreamers, shamans, and wise people, led by the sachem of the village in the council house. No longhouse had enough room for such a gathering, and now even the council house was full. Once again the two who had seen the vision recounted the experience to the wisest and most gifted of all the clans.

They were questioned even more intensely. When their tale was told, all about them sat gazing into the fire, giving the problem their most concentrated thought. Runs-Bucks felt he must rise and run yelling from the council house, as the meditation stretched into hours.

However, this session did not take as long as the last. Ayonhwatha, who was the chosen messenger of Wathadodarho, the sachem, rose to his feet after a relatively short time. "There must be great magic made here. There must be a talisman for the one who searches, made with all the power we can contrive. Only such a talisman can help one of us to pass through that place in the forest and go into the land to which Two-Moons has been taken.

"I have been given a small vision that tells me each of us, all the Dreamers of our village, must go into his own

51

Dream where he will find one item that must be put into the talisman. Whatever it may be, a feather, a stone, a bone, we must place within it a breath of our own orenda. This is what I have seen in the flames of the council fire."

He sat again, cross-legged between his fellows, and Wathadodarho nodded his approval of his words. Then the sachem turned to Odatsehe. "We must know the heart of the warrior we have lost. You are leader of her clan, grandfather and uncle of her people. Tell us of Two-Moons-in-the-Sky, her family, and her life."

The old man rose with great dignity and looked about at his peers. "I am the father of the mother of Two-Moons-in-the-Sky," he began. "Her name was Kowa-okton, Great Spirit, and she, too, was a Dreamer of great power."

He looked about as all nodded. There had never been doubt that his daughter, who had been given three names, during her lifetime, by the Matron of the clan, had borne this name at the end of her life.

"From the time of her birth, we could see without doubt that this was a child touched by the Master of Life. She dreamed truly, even when very young, yet when Walks-Up-the-Mountain asked her to be his wife, she consented, for he was one she respected. All our clan held him in esteem, for he was a good hunter, generous to all, and my daughter lived well. Three daughters were born to them, and one son who was taken away by a wolf, symbol of his father's clan, when he was very small.

"There was at that time a dispute with the Lenni Lenape, and we fought. Walks-Up-the-Mountain was captured on a raid, and he was given the Honorable Death because of his courage. In after years we guested the Lenni Lenape, who told us beautiful stories of his courtesy during the torture. His jokes, one said to me, had all attending upon him laughing. Then they wept to see the strength of his control during the ordeals.

"He died with honor, and they ate his flesh in order to

52

share in his strength. That was a great tribute, and we still value it. Something of his valor still runs among those old enemies, I am certain."

"Ohe," murmured Wathadodarho. "This is true."

"Upon his passing, my daughter began to dream again, and each dream she discussed with the Dreamers. At the first winter feasting, she was given the name Dreams-With-Truth. At that time she took up the use of weapons again, which she had discontinued upon becoming a wife.

"The women of the clan muttered, disturbed by such behavior, but the sachem at that time remembered other women who had taken up the task of becoming warriors and hunters. Though their number was not large, they all carried themselves well and with honor.

"So it was with my daughter. She served her clan and her village well, until the day when she spoke with a False-Face. After that she returned to the longhouse to die in her own place with her daughters about her."

There came a grunt from the listeners. Someone had not heard the tale before, Runs-Bucks decided. "Two-Moons-in-the-Sky was named because of a dream her mother had when the child was small. Not one of the other Dreamers could interpret this, though the oldest believed it was very important. He said that no one, even the Matron, should rename her, no matter how strong the reason.

"Being the eldest of the children, she cared for her small sisters. Taking up her mother's weapons, she practiced among the boys to develop great skill. In time, she hunted for her family, while her sisters tended the house-place.

"She too dreamed true, and her dreams have been a wonder and a worry to all the shamans and Dreamers since that time. Until now we have found no reasonable interpretations for them, but this vision revealed a shining opening into another place, as her dream did. One concerned a man of strange aspect, his face very white and his robe very black. Another revealed a longhouse set on end, with snow all around it.

"It is my thought that she has gone into that strange place, found that black longhouse and the white-faced man. This now is the tale of Two-Moons-in-the-Sky and her mother. Let us dream a way to find her, my brothers and sisters."

Odatsehe took his place again among his fellows, and silence fell about them, broken only by the snapping of the fire. They all stared into the flames, for the time had come, Runs-Bucks knew, to make great magic. They must create a talisman that could help him enter the world where Two-Moons had gone before him.

And then? He could not guess, but whatever came, he knew he must go after her into the unknown.

# CHAPTER SEVEN

## STRANGE WORLD, STRANGE WAYS

Two-Moons remained inside her hut long after dawn brightened the sky, for she knew the man would come at last to seek for her. She was not hiding from him, and she wanted him to understand that without question. Her message should have been clear—she would not endure captivity.

This morning the sun did not rise into view, for low clouds threatened even more snow. She was glad she did not need to hunt in such weather; shavings from the deer carcass gave her sustenance, although she did not relish raw meat. Munching on the shreds of venison, she waited and watched the tower, alert for any activity there.

At last the door opened and, as if it had been awaiting that signal, a bitter wind swept across the forest, riffled the layers on the ice, and brought with it the first gust of a new snowstorm. The black robe whipped behind Burning Hand as he came, and his uncovered head seemed inhumanly pale, for even his hair held no color. As the wind swirled it around his neck, Two-Moons thought of the False-Face of her own forests. Her mother had described just such a look as she lay dying.

Leaning into the wind, the tall black shape moved toward her across the ice and up the snowy stream bank. He did not come very near her hut but swung one arm toward her, then back toward the tower. That shelter now looked very warm and secure, as cold fingers of wind probed through the many chinks of her brush hut's walls.

"Come into the Tower, Woman," he called, though his words meant nothing to her. "I promise not to confine you again. There are matters that must be made clear between us if we are to work together." His words were distorted now by the wind and the swirling snow.

If his words meant nothing, his gestures did. He had come to make terms, it was quite clear.

Two-Moons moved forward on her knees and rose to her feet. Reaching back into the hut, she pulled out the remains of the deer and slung the carcass across her shoulder. She did not waste food, no matter what kinds Burning Hand might keep in his tall house.

As she approached, he stared at her and her burden as if he could not believe she was bringing her own food. Something about her—her look or her ways—seemed to puzzle him. That was just, she thought, for much about him puzzled her as well. She stepped past him, but he did not move to avoid her proximity. Sure-footed in her double-thick moccasins, she made her way across the ice to the door in the stone tower.

Before she remembered the way in which he had opened the closure, he caught up with her and pushed the door inward. Then he pointed a pale finger to his right and touched the deer. Ah, now she understood. There was a storage place for food there, down here in the chilly depths of the structure. She turned her steps toward the door he indicated. This one opened into a smaller room with stone floor and walls. Hooks hung from the walls and from thick timbers running across its ceiling, and on some hung skinned rabbits. A larger carcass was suspended from the biggest hook, and there was another large enough for the remnants of her deer.

The room was very cold, and she knew the meat would keep for a long while, if the weather did not turn warm. Even then, amid this thick stone, the chill might linger for many, many days.

Two-Moons looked about her as they emerged from the storage place. Where were his women? Or was he entirely alone here? He seemed to understand hunting, considering the rabbits and the other meat hung on the hooks, but he probably was not a warrior. He didn't carry himself like one used to weapons.

Perhaps he kept his own house, but she wondered how he made the stuff of which his clothing was fashioned. That would require skills she had never heard about. Filled with curiosity, she followed him up the steps again, into the upper reaches of the tower.

A third door opened from that landing that had led into his work room and into the chamber where she had eaten his food and left by his window. This one let them into a room filled with those leather-bound objects that had roused her curiosity the night before. She laid a hand on one lying on the table centering the room and looked at him questioningly. His pale eyes widened. "Book!" he said, with emphasis. "This is a book. Look—it contains many words, written down onto paper."

"Book," she repeated, staring at the thing. "Book."

He opened the book and held it out to her, so she could see the markings on its yellowish pages. She took it in cautious hands, for it seemed to contain strong magic. It had the feel of magic, and when she looked down, it held markings that were not pictures like those her own kind used to record their history and their battles.

The marks were not random scratches, like those made by children drawing in the sand with sticks. These marks obviously meant something, and she was impatient with herself that she did not instantly divine their meaning.

She laid it carefully on the table and moved toward the

fire. She sat on a low stool before the blaze, for her feet were chilled, even through the doubled moccasins. She drew off the first moccasin and laid it to in the warmth.

Behind her, his voice said, "Shoe."

She glanced back to make sure what he meant, and he was pointing at the moccasin. She laid her hand on it and said, "Ahta," giving the thing a shake as she spoke. "Shoo."

He seemed excited now, moving about the room, lifting things and naming them. For many of those items she had no corresponding word, for her people made nothing like them. Yet she watched and listened intently, memorizing most of the words he gave her. Before both grew weary, they shared many words for things and even some for actions.

She had never done anything quite like this before, for the tribes living near the Onondaga spoke variations on the basic Iroquois-Huron tongue. A Nihatientakona could understand a Lenni Lenape. A Huron could speak with an Onondaga. Only the dreaded Algonkians, sometimes captured when raiding into her own country, did not share their common language, and even their tongue had some similarities with hers.

Before long, they sat, silent, on either side of the table, looking at one another with eyes that had grown wary again. They were of kinds so extremely different that she could not guess what to expect from him, and she knew the same was true when he thought about her.

She had no reason to trust him. He had, after all, brought her out of her own place without her consent and for an unknown purpose. Deep inside herself, she felt that she would not approve of his purposes, if she ever decided what they might be. Unconsciously, she shivered.

As if reading her thoughts, Burning Hand rose and added fuel to the fire. Then he led her back into the room where he had left her the night before. There was fire there, rebuilt and burning brightly.

He gestured for her to enter, and then he stared at her intently before turning to go into that other door that led into the room where she had watched him in her vision. It seemed a very long time since Aireskoi had led her disembodied spirit there to gaze at him as he set his traps. When he was gone, she shut the door, for a terrible draft moved through the tower, drawing up the long shaft toward some opening at the top. Then she sat before the fire and gazed into the flames, reaching inward toward the place where lived the part of her that was totally a Dreamer. For she was remembering a dream she had long ago, when she was a small child.

There, too, had been a doorway into an alien place. Why had she not recognized this last as such a one? I could not see it, because of the snow, she thought. I could not feel it because I was so weary and so cold.

The path she had followed so easily, even though it was hidden under its white blanket, had been one her inner self...recognized? Why hadn't her spirit cried out in recognition when she first stepped into this place?

She had seen that tower, blurred as if in a dream, very long ago when her mother still lived. She had seen a man, also, and Burning Hand must be the one in her dream.

She let out a long sigh. So, she had been given a sign, even so very long ago. Such were signs that were never the sole concern of those to whom they were given.

Dreamers might struggle and live—or struggle and die—without bringing forth such a vision. One person was given such a dream for a reason beyond her own welfare, for such visions were given to the tribe or the clan. If she had been warned then, it was because the warning concerned the welfare of her people.

"Aireskoi," she murmured. "Taonhiawagi!" Her spirit reached out, seeking for a vision, but there came no whisper in her mind and no sound in the room beyond the mutter of the fire in the fire-hole.

There remained the possibility of Dream. It was just past mid-day, though the low-hanging cloud made it seem much darker and later. She was not sleepy, but she knew she must send herself into dream, if she was to understand what was happening to her and what might endanger her people.

For the second time, she laid herself upon the bed-place and covered herself with her robe. Closing her eyes, she sent herself winging down the dark tunnel that led to sleep....

* * * * * * *

Two-Moons almost cried out with joy. Once more she was among the trees in her own land, at a spot on the path leading to the village. The sun shone upon the snow, and she could hear the voices of children in the distance, amid the barking of dogs. Here was the elm against which she had leaned. Beside it was a brush hut much like the one she had made in the forest outside the tower. She drifted toward it, realizing that she had no body in this place when no footmark marred the snow as she passed.

She bent to peer into the door hole. In the shadowy recess she saw a big dark shape wrapped in bearskin. The eyes were closed in the coppery face—and it was Runs-Bucks-Down. He was seeking for her, she knew, here where the elm held the touch of her shoulder and her hand. He had made his shelter here and was seeking a vision to guide him to her.

He had always been her true friend, as well as her husband who might have been. Knowing the strength of his orenda and the stubbornness of his will, she did not doubt he would achieve his vision. Yet how might he follow her, even if he somehow learned about the trap that had been set beyond this place?

Again she drifted, and the forest thinned about her. Now she stood in another place, unlike any she had ever seen. She stood upon a stone embankment, a thing made by men, for the stones were square and smooth, like those of Burning Hand's tower. Beyond her, the land dropped away into a cupped valley, whose grasses were a deep blue-green and whose trees were small and slender, like birches, yet alien-looking. Their leaves were almost as blue as the sky of her own world.

She looked upward to find this sky yellowish. The sun was almost upon the horizon before her, and two pale ghost-moons hung in that sky. One was directly overhead, the other rising, she found as she turned to look behind her.

She had seen the moon of her own world shining palely as the sun set. And here there were two moons in the sky, in truth, as her mother had seen them in that long ago dream. Had she come into the world of her mother's Dream?

Shaken, she closed her intangible eyes for an instant. When she opened them again, she was in still another place, surrounded by walls of gleaming stuff unlike stone or wood or hide. The walls surrounded a town, as did the wall around her village of longhouses. Many people stood in the space contained within those walls. In the center of that space a platform had been raised high, so that whoever stood there could be seen by all inside the wall.

Someone stood there now, pale and tall and thin like Burning Hand. He wore a robe dyed blue, and he held in his hand an axe made of the same shining stuff as the knife with which Burning Hand had cut her meat. Drawn by curiosity, she wafted forward, finding to her surprise that she had no need to avoid those standing in her way. She could move through them at will, and they never knew she had touched them. It was very strange!

At the foot of the platform stood a rank of chiefs, identified as such by their bearing and their rich clothing. They also gazed upward toward the man in blue, and she turned her gaze there, also. Across a slab before him lay another man, his head laid into a depression in the stone, his face turned away, so she could not see it.

Something about that figure was familiar.

The axe man raised his tool high, and a woman among the watchers cried out in grief and covered her eyes. The axe fell, the blow powerful to sever the neck below with one strike—but the man was no longer there. Amid a quiver of light, he had, quite simply, disappeared.

Two-Moons looked around her. The tallest of the men in the ranks of chiefs shouted with anger, though she could not understand his words. The axe man dropped his axe to clatter on the stone below the platform and sat on the slab, his limbs shaking visibly.

The woman cried out again, this time with obvious joy, and the crowd began to draw away, as if fearing some unknown danger.

She thought she understood why, for never had she seen such fury as lay upon the face of the tallest chief. Those about him also emitted cries of rage and a heat of passion quite tangible to her present state of being. A wrongdoer had been there for punishment. Not the Honorable Death but a more ignominious fate. In some way he had been taken away from this place and deposited—where?

Even as she had been. She examined the thought and nodded.

Now she moved again, into a place so full of sun and warmth that even her bodiless spirit reveled in it. She was in a room not unlike that in the tower, though this was much larger and open to the air and sunlight. Two men stood in the center of the room, their eyes focused upon an empty spot between them. She could feel their effort, the working of their wills as they strove to accomplish some esoteric task.

Something acrid burned within the room—even without nostrils, she could smell it. Books lay scattered about, and another was in the hand of the smaller of the two men. He looked at it now and again, speaking words as if he gained knowledge of them from the pages in his hand.

It occurred to Two-Moons that the marks must be words, something like the symbols by means of which the wise men recorded the deeds of the Onondaga. With exact words, knowledge might be passed from person to person over long spans of time, even though the ones who might tell of it might die.

Smoke and steam, or something very like both, began to fill the space between the two men. As they frowned with concentration, the smoke curdled, becoming solid and shaping itself into a man. A man she recognized. Blinking with surprise, a younger Burning Hand stood there; his hands were tied behind him, his black robe wrinkled and torn, spattered with refuse, as if those in the crowd had flung things at him as he lay on the platform. He fell forward, and the larger man caught him and laid him upon a bench.

The small man moved quickly to a table and poured something from a jug into a container as clear as spring water. He held this to the lips of the black-robed man, and he sipped, choked, and sipped again. The stuff seemed to hearten him, for he sat up straighter and looked around him.

Two-Moons realized that he must understand something about what had been done to him, for he was asking questions, though it was obvious his listeners did not understand his words any more than she could. When he held out his bound hands behind him, twisting awkwardly to do so, the smaller man, after a wary glance at his fellow, took up a bright-bladed knife and cut the cord that held them.

Burning Hand stretched out his arms and laughed

aloud. His gaze traveled around the room, as if he sought to see everything it contained at once. Those watching him laughed, too, though there was a strange note in their voices. Two-Moons drifted toward them, feeling sure she would not be seen. They owned faces she would never like to trust, she thought, gazing into first one set of dark, wrinkle-lidded eyes, then into the other. Those faces seemed pinched, the faces of men who feared many things and resented their own fear. They were the faces of men who would do dishonorable things in order to gain their wills.

They were warped faces...False-Faces?

With that thought, she found herself once more inside her own body, lying on the bed-place and listening to the dim flutter of the fire in the tower room. She had seen her own home, her friend Runs-Bucks-Down. She had seen, it was clear, the place where Burning Hand belonged, and it was not this place. As well, she believed she had witnessed the act that brought him into this world from that in which two moons rode the summer sky.

# CHAPTER EIGHT

## REMEMBERING MOROR

Lallius kept his distance from his captive, not seeking her out again that day. Aside from feeling cautious about her possibly dangerous abilities, he was also in a quandary about dealing with her. The ways in which he had dealt with women in both his pasts, the one here and the older one on Moror—would obviously not work with this unusual and determined female. From the first she had made that clear, past any barrier posed by lack of a common language.

He kept to his laboratory, studying his books, cleaning his equipment, and pondering his problem. In mid-afternoon he heard the ancient wood of the landing creak beneath her soft step as she passed his door and started down the stair. He crept from his room and listened as she made her way down and, by straining his ears, he could hear the door to the larder open. She had obviously gone after food, and he found himself hungry. Would she bring something to prepare for him as well? He had no confidence that she understood her female functions well enough to do that as a matter of course.

The soft step returned and did not falter before entering the room he had prepared for his guest. She would roast meat over her fire, he guessed, and be satisfied with that. He was in better condition as he seared his meat over the flames of his spirit lamps, holding the strips with crucible tongs so as not to burn his fingers. Sighing, he went down to secure his own supply of meat.

He prepared his meal as quietly as possible. For some reason, he did not want her to know he was engaged in the menial task of cookery, though he had cooked for himself for a century now. He needed slaves for that and for other purposes, and that had been his motivation in setting a trap for a primitive.

That trap had succeeded—or had it? He could see no way in which he could use this intractable woman to help him secure more of her people for that purpose.

As night fell, the storm grew worse, wind slashing snow against the shutters in violent whispers of chill and damp. His trip to the garde-robe was a horror of cold blasts on his bare bottom and cold stone beneath his slippered feet. Glad to reach his chamber again, he built up his meager fire. Dropping into the sagging chair before the fireplace, he relaxed in his night robe, huddled in a coverlet from his bed. Staring into the flames, he pondered the problem, but his mind seemed singularly empty of ideas. If only Master Albertus were here to help him, he thought. Even his old master on his home world, who had taught him the things that brought him, at last, to the headsman's block, might have been a useful source of information.

Condrille had been his first teacher in the arcane arts. Condrille had been horrified when Lallius asked him questions about matters his youthful imagination considered. Unlike Albertus, Condrille had confined his studies and his experimentations to positive aspects of the esoterica, and he had discouraged his pupils from looking into any of their negative applications.

Lallius, whose name in that place was Osperre, soon learned to dig on his own into the thick and dusty scrolls in Condrille's library. During his investigations, he found that Condrille's predecessors had not been so finicky. They had not been content with the nobler aspects of their calling, but had discovered matters that made even his diamond-edged spirit quail when he found them written onto the faded parchments. He copied the more abstruse and interesting ones for later use. Even as his quill scratched the words onto his own tablet, he felt a tingle in his fingers, as if some demonic spirit were even then being released, merely by the act of writing.

The feeling did not frighten him. On the contrary, it excited him, for he had been a strange one, even as a boy. His parents had begun to suspect his unusual qualities early in his life. In his fifth year, all the fowl in the run seemed to develop a strange disease that left them drooping and dispirited. Only when the cook found a wound beneath the feathers of one destined for the table did the adults realize that something was draining blood from the poultry at night.

Sitting in his grimy chair, he almost smiled, remembering the dusty-feather stink of the hen-runs, the drowsy quarreling of the chickens on their roosts. There had been a dilemma, the first time, of what to do with the blood. All his instincts told him that it was valuable, in some as yet undiscovered way, and he had hidden the full basin under his bed.

Days later the stench was too terrible to bear. He poured it away down the stream that ran through the garden, in the wee hours of the morning. Something within him had mourned the waste. One day, he would know what to do with blood, he knew even then.

Many years later, while looking into Condrille's scrolls, he had discovered what his inner self had longed to do. And that was when his real trouble had begun.

Hens are one thing, useful but not valued for themselves. A sister was something entirely different, he discovered. When his parents discovered Susilla, after searching for hours along the stream-crossed meadows beyond their home, she was as pale as building stone. There was no sign of an attack. Her clothing was neatly arranged about her, her hands lying peacefully at her sides. But there was no missing the terrible wound in her throat. There was talk that some animal had come down from the forested slopes beyond the valley to attack her as she dozed beside the stream.

That had almost made young Osperre laugh aloud, although he had learned long before to maintain a sober demeanor. He sensed that his elders did not quite believe their own explanations. Whatever their inner convictions, all kept their children close by their own gardens, and it became impossible to find unattended youngsters in the meadows after that.

It had been his sister's blood that brought him first into contact with Those Others who lived apart from the visible world. Long years and another world later, Albertus had called them demons, but Lallius understood that they were not what the church-taught magus had thought them to be. They lived in no lake of fire between calls from adepts. They lived, instead, outside all physical things except when it interested them to enter the world for their own purposes. They were not actually wicked, as Albertus had thought of such things. But they were untiringly curious and meddlesome, amused by the small men who thought to control them with patterns in chalk and words spoken in dead tongues. They held nothing in common with humankind, either the people of Moror or of Europe.

Condrille would have been horrified if he had known what esoteric ingredients his young pupil smuggled into his laboratory, after the old man had gone to his rooms for the night. He would have been terrified to see some of the results brought about by the boy's manipulations of the ingredients he brought there in secret.

Lallius had learned early that dead creatures of all

kinds seemed to fascinate them. He had never known why that was true, though he wondered if, being deathless, they were intrigued by death itself. Blood always drew them, and that was likewise understandable. They had nothing like it and seemed envious of those who possessed it.

He learned, using different recipes and incantations, to catch the interest of different sorts of that invisible and elusive kind. He had dreamed that they called themselves the Klathe, although he could never prove his dream was correct. All the while Condrille grew older, and he never suspected that Osperre was not all that a young man should be. When he was satisfied that he had taught his student all he needed to know, he retired to his villa in the forested hills, leaving Osperre to serve as teacher to aspiring mages and adviser to the Royal Family.

Lallius found it amazing how different his two worlds had been in their approach to magic. In Moror, magic was something one used as he did water and air and light and darkness. It was a natural matter, made for the use of mankind. Here it was secret, hidden, and dangerous to profess, but those who ruled nations did not neglect the potencies it could provide them. Although they were taught to fear and hate it, they used mages and adepts to work their wills, though their own laws taught them to destroy those who used those arts.

Lallius sighed as his fire died low and rose from his chair. Before burning low, the fire had warmed his sleeping room. He lay upon his couch and pulled his bedclothes about him, while a flicker of ruddy light danced on the ceiling among the cobwebs. That light reminded him of the flame that had burned beneath the Great Crucible. That had been the culmination of his career, he knew, even after so many years of effort. Nothing he could ever achieve would approach it for daring, for research, and for knowledge.

Only one as young as he had been then, who had not

yet realized his own mortality, would have dared to venture upon such a project. Whatever the attitudes might be in Moror toward sorcerous activities, there were still powerful families with whom one did not meddle.

The Royal Family should have headed the list of those. So sacred were the persons of the royal couple and their offspring that it never occurred to them (or to anyone else) that some nefarious sorcerer might dare to use one of the family in a necromantic endeavor.

To be truthful, it would never have occurred to Osperre, either, without the death of the Royal Infant. He had been called to attend the sick girl-child, as had every spell-caster and physician in the kingdom and even beyond the principal city. Osperre had done his best, as had they all, and yet he had been secretly relieved when all his incantations and all his potions did not cause the waxen shape of the child to show any sign of recovery.

He had seen such illness before, and always it left the sufferer bereft of his wits, if he survived at all. It was better to die, he had always thought, than to live as an idiot.

From listening to their whispers, he knew his peers felt the same. If she lived, that infant would become ruler of Moror's largest continent, succeeding her parents. Such a damaged ruler always led to intrigues and the establishment of power-cliques that always disrupted the peaceful government of the country. This had happened every time unfit rulers acceded to the throne.

It was with considerable relief that the healers found themselves sent home by the grieving parents, for they knew death would come soon. Before long, the death was announced by sentinels blowing their long wooden horns, whose mellow voices sent the word across the city and into the countryside.

The mournful noise waked Osperre from an uneasy slumber. He raised himself on one elbow to listen to its message. At that moment his fatal idea was born, fostered by a dream left over from the night. In that last, best sleep of morning, when a man knows he should rise and go about his work, yet finds no immediate need to leave his warm nest, he had dreamed of that potent corpse, which was even then being washed in the holy spring and dressed in white. If one could summon Those Others with the dead flesh of a beast, how much more potent bait might be the body of a royal child?

That dream had frightened him, and he woke covered with sweat, though the morning was cool. The girl who shared his bed felt his unease too, and opened her eyes to stare at him. Then she fled to the dressing closet, where he could hear her hurrying on her garments with mad haste.

"It was only a dream," he said aloud, more to himself than to her. Yet he could not forget that vision.

Before noon all those who had attended the dead infant were called to sit with her small body in the Room of Waking. By turns they kept guard, that none might become too weary. Osperre had entered the glass-walled temple with his eyes cast down, not in sorrow but in fear that anyone meeting his gaze might read therein some hint of his purpose. No one had, and at last he was left alone with the infant. Even now, lying in his own bed in another world, he shuddered to think what he had done. He had wrapped the still shape in its white swaddlings and tucked it into his robe. Then he had slipped away from the Room of Waking through a rear door and fled through the town, taking the child's body to his own laboratory, which he had set up amid the farms north of the city.

He could still see the tiny hands, stiff with death, pale with the wasting disease that had taken the small life. The little face was quiet and benign as he prepared the Great Crucible, which he had shaped and tempered for other projects less important than this.

He had added the ingredients found in those unholy recipes copied over the years. He had brought that awful broth to a boil and lowered into it the body of the child. The waxen eyelids opened, and the face wrinkled into fury and despair. The child shrieked aloud.

He still felt the grip of despair he had felt then. The child had been truly dead. There had been no mistake. Yet the thing he did to her body, at the peril of her spirit, had moved the mortal clay to one last protest. Faint as it was, that cry gained force and rang through the fields, past the houses of farmers and craftsmen, through the city itself. Those who heard it understood that something dreadful was taking place, and those other healers suspected what it might be. They led retribution down upon their erstwhile colleague, furious that one who called himself their equal had seized power he was unfit to wield.

The experiment had, of course, been an unqualified success, for no fewer than three powerful Presences had attended him at once. By then, however, he had only one thing to beg: "Save me, Masters, from the fruits of my folly!"

Those misty faces looming in the dark room full of stenches and miasmas had laughed. Then the largest one, the most hideous and jeering one, spoke. "You will be saved from the headsman, Osperre, if only because you dared so much to attract our notice. Your life will still be yours, and it will be very long before it moves into any dimension we know. Yet it may be that before you die you will consider this no favor and no kindness, and long life will become a burden you would willingly forgo."

For weeks, lying in the dank prison, he had lived with the fear of his own death, while the wheels of the law turned deliberately and the twin moons moved in their orbits. Men and women who had feared even to speak his name had come to his cell to cast rotten fruits at him and to shout hateful words.

He had been powerless to protect himself. It seemed that terrible act he had performed had drained him of all his hard-won potencies. He could not cast so much as a spark to illuminate the darkness, although that was the simplest of tricks. Condrille had taught him to cast light from his fingers when he first came as a child to study with the wizard.

At last the dreaded day arrived, but by then he had lost all hope that those Presences might come to his aid. Surely they would have prevented such suffering, such insult, such fear to plague their devotee, if they had intended to save him.

Angry and distraught as they had been, the Royal Family had him washed and dressed in fresh black, as fitted one of his rank. When the jailer came for him, he managed to walk out of the prison without his knees failing him, though afterward he hardly knew how. When the cart deposited him on the platform, he had dropped to his knees and bowed his face into his hands.

As if this act of contrition eased their anger, the people stopped casting offal at him and ceased their shouting. They waited, eyes bright and alert in the strong light of the marketplace.

The executioner led him to the block and arranged his limbs in the approved position. As if another will moved him, he complied, controlling his bowels and his expression with equal determination. He heard a swish as the terrible axe was raised above him, and he had closed his eyes tightly, waiting. There came a moment of disorientation, and he felt a chill gust of air seize his body and carry him away.

At the last moment, he thought with wild glee, "THEY keep their word. I am saved!" Then he was—elsewhere. There on his hard couch in the tower, Lallius pulled the covers up to his chin.

Wind blasted against the outer wall and sent thin slivers of icy air into his chamber. It battered his window as if to enter his rooms and root him from his secure nest. Shivering, he closed his eyes yet again, hoping to be delivered from this terrible sentence Those Others had carried out.

He had thought himself the most fortunate of men, when he found himself safe in the chambers of Albertus Parvus, here in a world he knew must be other than the one he had known all his life. This had similarities, but the light was a different color, the weight of his body on his legs was subtly greater, and the shapes and colors of the leaves fluttering outside the wide windows were not those of leaves he knew.

The moment of translation was, he now knew, the high point of his life. Escape was sweet, and when he realized that he was in the presence of one of the three most powerful mages of this new world, ambition waked again within him. A burning desire to learn all this new world could teach him had sent him forward, although now he would have traded everything for a warm climate, with servants or slaves to serve him, giving him rest and time to think and work.

The wind chuckled wickedly against the wall. He shivered, wondering if death could possibly have been as terrible as he had thought, when he was young and ignorant of the misery attendant upon age.

# CHAPTER NINE

## MAKING A TALISMAN

The creation of a talisman could not be done carelessly or quickly, Runs-Bucks knew. Though he chafed at waiting upon his peers to find their own parts of the thing, he was thankful that his impatience would not influence the deliberations of Odatsehe and Wathadodarho. The two elders knew that any careless step might well doom Two-Moons to a lifetime in that unknown place to which she had been drawn. Knowing that, the Dreamer held his own spirit with iron control, and continued to wait.

All the clans of the village—the Wolf, the Bear, the Deer, and the Tortoise—were involved in this effort, their dreamers and elders busy divining the items that would be their own contributions to the talisman. The first step in that process was fasting, for before anyone could dream with full effectiveness, he or she must clear body and mind of earthly matters.

After the fasting, the False-Face society performed its rituals, insuring that none of the demonic faces could linger around the village, tainting the work they must do. Their masks and drums and their gourd rattles came out of ancient hiding places, the dances and chants were performed, and that bit of business was done at last. Only then did the Dreamers go to their own special places for dreaming and open themselves to the visions that might come. Runs-Bucks went, as he usually did, to the forest, even though it was locked in the grip of this terrible winter.

There was a place where the small stream that watered the village ran into a larger one, which in turn flowed into the lake his people called the Skaneateles. Through a deep, narrow gorge, the stream fell over a cliff into a pot-like hole worn into the solid stone. Now the fall looked like fangs of ice, some of them extending from the top of the fall into the sheet of ice at the bottom, but even in the most terrible cold some water continued to trickle beneath the ice.

In summer, ferns grew along the banks, twining among flowers and vines, to make a magical dell of the spot. There he had gone as a boy to have visions and dream dreams. Those were not the important visions of adulthood that foretold dangers and vital necessities; they had been the softer visions of youth. He had dreamed himself the greatest hunter of the tribe for an entire afternoon. He had climbed Oneonta, the mountain of his people, which he had been forbidden to climb until he was older. There he had made himself a great messenger, bearer of wampum to the chiefs of the Kanonsionni.

It had been there where he had spoken his heart to Two-Moons. Her refusal had been so gentle, so filled with affection and pain, that it had not made the place bitter to him. Indeed, now it was to him the most sacred of all the spots he knew in all the lands of his fathers.

"A warrior cannot risk growing heavy with child," she had said, her voice quiet and stern with her discipline. "A warrior cannot allow his skills to grow dull while she digs in the ground or tends to things needed about the home." She had sighed and looked up into his eyes intently.

"And a Dreamer—you know, Runs-Bucks, that we must keep our minds clear of minor matters, however important they may seem for a day or an hour. We must be channels through which messages and warnings can pour in order to insure the welfare of our people.

"Dearly though I would love to do it, I cannot ask you to move into my quarters. Yet I will always be your friend and brother, and never will we quarrel. We will never allow our paths to move in opposite directions, unless Taonhiawagi wills it." He could almost hear her soft voice as he descended into the frozen dell.

Flowers of frost and ice filled it now, and it was as beautiful, in this guise, as it had been in summer. Bright drops fell lazily from icicles fringing the outfall of the smaller stream, and the muffled pat of their impact on the snow-covered ice below was the only thing breaking the quiet.

Runs-Bucks laid aside his bearskin robe and his buckskin under-cloak. Clad only in his sleeveless shirt, breechclout, and leggings, he sat cross-legged in the snow. Folding his arms, he closed his eyes and pulled all his senses inward. The chill bite against his skin drifted away as his consciousness drifted away and the sound of the dripping faded.

His mind shrank inside his skull to the size of a nut, a berry. And then it expanded again, finding inside his spirit wide reaches filled with white mists that swirled as if a breeze moved them.

Runs-Bucks floated forward into the mists and across the spaces. As he moved, objects came into view, half-veiled by the vapors. There were trees unlike those he knew, rocks that were different from those found in the forests and hills of his own place. A tall shape, black and narrow, stood in the white mist, and he felt a jolt of excitement beneath his breastbone. He felt the presence of Two-Moons, as if she stood before him.

He approached the place, and now he knew that another stream than the one he knew flowed beside him, under thick ice. The long shape ahead was a dark blur against the snow, when suddenly a light flashed from a square opening high up in its side, blazing brightly across the darkness.

Runs-Bucks was suddenly very near, gazing up at this strange longhouse, which stood on an island in the stream. The ice was frozen hard, and he went across, knowing that here he had no body to crush through, if it should be thin. He found a door-place stopped with wood. When he touched it, his fingers sank into the material as if it—or he—were not actually there at all. He laid his head on his hand, sorrowing that he might not go in, but as his gaze dropped to the snow at his feet he saw a small moccasin print.

Beside it lay something else. He knelt in the snow and looked at the small image lying half buried in a drift. It was the likeness of a warped face, carved in blue stone. He recognized it instantly as a False-Face, just as they had been described to him, but this one only as large as his thumbnail.

As he touched it, his fingers tingled, and he knew this must be his own contribution to the contents of the talisman. He groped through the stone image without disturbing the snow about it. How could he take it back with him to the spot where his body waited?

He sat back on his heels and thought. There must be a way, for he had been led here to find just this thing. It was clear, then, that there had to be some way in which he could lift it from this spot and carry it back with him to his body in the dell.

Squatting in the snow, bodiless, unfeeling, intangible, he knew he must wait for a sign. That was all he could think of that might help him. Time crept slowly past, but the white mist never varied in intensity. There was never any change in the light, no hint that the sun might rise or set. All about him seemed frozen to total stillness, as he waited there.

Then he became aware that his fingers had begun to glow, very dimly like fireflies in summer meadows. His right hand grew warmer, and he realized that except for that initial tingle, this was the first physical sensation he had known since sinking into his trance beside the waterfall.

With those glowing fingers, he reached for the stone face. As he touched it there came a sharper tingle, as if the thing knew his touch and dreaded it. Nevertheless, he was able to grasp and lift it.

Then he was swept back, as though by a wind that could neither be felt nor heard, to the place where his body waited. He was within his skin again, opening his eyes. The sun was setting, making the icy treetops flash and glitter as the wind stirred them.

He looked down at his right hand. There lay the Face, too small for the strangeness it contained. As blue as the shadows lying on snow in twilight, it stared up at him as grimly as he stared down at it.

For a breathless moment there was a connection between the two of them. Runs-Bucks felt it holding his gaze as something strong, imprisoned within that small shape, shouted to his spirit, demanding something he could not understand and would not grant if he knew it.

He closed his fingers about it and tucked it into his pouch. Then he began flexing, warming his muscles after he donned his robes again. It was risky to leave the body in such cold, but all seemed to be well. Soon he was trudging back through the growing darkness toward the longhouse of his clan.

When he pushed back the deer-hide door covering, he saw that Odatsehe was sitting beside the central fire already, his legs crossed, arms folded, eyes closed, still in the grip of his vision. Without speaking, Runs-Bucks moved to sit beside the clan-chief, arrange his limbs, and gaze into the flames.

Only when the older man grunted did Runs-Bucks venture to speak. "I have brought a thing, Clan-Father, for the making of the talisman. I would like to give it into your keeping, for it contains fearful omens."

The gnarled brown hand opened, and he dropped the blue-glowing stone image into it. Odatsehe gasped, a short controlled jolt of breath, as it touched his skin. Then he was silent, as if trying to read the thing through feeling it in his hand.

They sat there for a time, and then Okton-iyo came to join them, sitting on the other side of Odatsehe. When the Clan-chief acknowledged his presence, he laid a lump of stained wood into his hand, without speaking or even looking at it.

One by one the Dreamers of the Tortoise Clan, the Wolf, the Bear, and the Deer Clans came into the long-house, back from their dreaming. Each set into the hand of the fruit of his or her efforts, and when the last had arrived, the old man rose to stand before them.

He gazed around the circle, looking into the eyes of each person there. "This is the tally of our efforts, and there are many things here that contain orenda. There is one that contains much power of a kind we cannot understand. Runs-Bucks brought it, and I would know from what place it came into his hand."

He rose to his feet, his heart racing now, and told the tale of his vision. When he was done, Odatsehe held up the carven face to the others might see. In the firelight, it seemed to change its expression; as the fire flickered, the lines graven into the face seemed to move and deepen.

The members of the False-Face Society had gathered in a larger circle behind the Dreamers, and now they caught their breaths so sharply it sounded like one single gasp. This, Runs-Bucks knew, was a face so like those upon the masks they used in their rituals that it chilled their hearts. Just such a face, all his people understood, might appear to anyone who walked in the forest, withering his or spirit and body to the point of death.

Okton-iyo raised his head, his faded eyes flashing in the firelight. "This has come from that other place to which we saw the doorway," he said, his voice firm and unwavering. "Beyond that door we saw, Runs-Bucks, this had its beginning, and in itself it is a talisman. With it you can surely gain entrance to that other world to which Two-Moons has gone."

He stared at the image and shook his white head. "This was a strong dream, nephew, that you have had."

"Perhaps I should go now and see if it will take me through the doorway," Runs-Bucks suggested.

Odatsehe looked at him sternly and shook his head. "Of what use is it to enter if you cannot wield power there? Or if you cannot return? The other parts of the talisman will give to you part of the orenda of the entire tribe.

"Do not take this lightly, for such power is of the spirit and it is a wonderful thing. It is in my heart that you may need all this and more, if you go into that place to aid Two-Moons. If you are to help her return, you will need all of the talisman, for its parts tie you firmly to our own place, allowing you to come back when your task is done.

"Our brother Two-Moons has no such magical helper. You will need this for both of you."

Runs-Bucks looked down, ashamed. He deserved the rebuke, for his impatience had driven him, not his wits. His people knew that the impulsive nature of youth must be balanced by the mature deliberation of age, or the tribe could never flourish.

"Tomorrow all parts of the talisman will be gathered from all the clans. Then the sachem, all the shamans, and the Clan-Fathers will put them together with proper songs and rituals to make it powerful. After that, Runs-Bucks-

Down, you may seek out the place of that shining door-way."

He said nothing. No one objected that he had been chosen to do this thing, for all knew the special bond that tied him to Two-Moons, though they said nothing of that. It was his place to go after her into that other place, where he might find the Place of False-Faces as well.

This was no task that even the bravest craved to take from him, and Runs-Bucks did not reprove them for that. He would not have chosen the task for himself, had things been otherwise. Yet now he felt as he did before a raid; his heart was pounding, his body and spirit were afire with impatience to get on with the matter at hand.

As if reading his mind, Wathadodarho entered the clan-house and came to stand beside Odatsehe. "All is well with the Tortoise Clan?" he asked politely.

Odatsehe nodded gravely. "Except for this one small matter, all is well with us," he said. "Will you sit beside our fire and smoke with us?"

Wathadodarho folded himself into position, his limbs as flexible as those of one much younger. Taking the pipe, he puffed twice and passed it to the next in the circle. Then he said, "It is in my mind that the man you have chosen will need counsel from the shamans. He will need purifi-cation of body and spirit. He will need all the strength and wisdom our tribe is able to provide for him."

Odatsehe glanced at Runs-Bucks. "That is true," he said. "We have chosen this one, for his dream showed us that doorway. Runs-Bucks-Down is the chosen of the Tor-toise Clan."

Wathadodarho paused politely. Then he spoke with grave courtesy. "Then, my brother, will you allow me to take him for this night, so the wisest of the tribe may ad-vise him?" Odatsehe touched Runs-Bucks lightly upon his shoulder. "Go with the sachem, Great-Nephew. We will see you tomorrow, when the talisman is completed."

The young man rose with Wathadodarho and left the longhouse after him. He felt as if he were still in a dream, caught in a vision, for the concentrated orenda of all the wise men of the tribe seemed to wrap about him, while they moved through the snowy night to the longhouse of the Deer Clan.

# CHAPTER TEN

## THE HOMEWARD PATH

At last the blizzard blew itself out, leaving the tower standing hip-deep in a waste of snow. The stream was invisible beneath that white blanket, and even the growth along its banks was so burdened that it was hard to know where it had been. Only by the flatter expanse where the water had flowed could Two-Moons see where the stream lay.

Beyond it the wood loomed, black as the tower, and downstream the forest on either side of the river showed her the way she had come. She was not foolish enough to think that while the storm raged she could retrace her steps to the place where she had stepped into this new world.

For days, confined in the tower by weather, she had worked with the white-faced man, learning his words and teaching him her own. Except for that first night, there had been no friction—no obvious disagreement—between them. He had indicated that he wanted her to cook his meat, as if she had been his wife. That irritated her, even more so because she had no words to explain to him the reasons why she could be no man's woman or wife. As they argued, he used all the words they had shared, along with gestures that made his meaning quite clear.

In her turn, Two-Moons had spoken patiently at first, and then sharply. At last she was forced to invent a dance to convey her meaning, in which she showed herself engaged in battle with invisible enemies. That elicited from Burning-hand his word for war, and at last he seemed to understand what she was trying to say.

"War. Soldier. Warrior." He took the knife from the table and held it defensively, then thrust it at her in mock attack. "One who fights with other men. Yes?"

She stood before him, and as he thrust she swept the knife from his hand easily, without touching its blade. Then she showed him how to hold a knife in combat, swaying and slashing as she had done when actually engaged in battle. At last, pointing to herself, she said, "Soldier. Warrior," as he had done.

"You? How can that be?" His voice, which she was learning to read, sounded surprised.

"Onkwe ikiaks," she said, moving the knife suggestively. "I cut men. I shoot them with arrows, in time of war. I hunt for bear and deer and smaller beasts. I fish in the streams with the other men. I am not a woman, Burning-hand. You must not think of me as one."

Though he could not have understood all her words, she knew that he had grasped enough to trouble him greatly. He no longer expected her to cook for him, though when she smelled the result of his cookery wafting from his laboratory, she understood his need for someone else to prepare his food. They had gone forward through the days of the blizzard, not easily but without overt friction. When the snow stopped, Two-Moons looked out of the lower doorway, staring down the stream toward the place from which she had come. She knew Burning-hand would not let her go without protest—perhaps he might even make physical attempts to control her. Though she felt confident that she could conquer him, for he was woefully unskilled at anything that required strength or flexibility, she was uncertain about his magical skills. He might be able to call upon powers that even Aireskoi could not control.

Pretending merely to be interested in the weather, she turned and went up the stair to her room again. There she took up one of the books containing drawings of beasts and birds, men and weapons, tools and houses. Slowly she was learning to decipher the markings beneath them, faded and spidery though they seemed, and turn them into the words Burning-hand taught her. She thought he was pleased with her learning that written tongue, though he said nothing about it.

Morning wore away to noon, and she heard the man go heavily down the steps to the place where he kept his meat. She felt somewhat disdainful of his need for eating three times a day; for one of her people, particularly for warriors, once was enough. Only young children needed food so often.

When he returned, she waited and soon smelled the stink of his scorching meat. That was as bad as the less recognizable but subtly nasty odors that came from the room when he worked there. She had wondered a great deal about what he did there, but his interests were so alien to her that she had come to no conclusion. He worked magic, she knew. But why? No one seemed to threaten him in this tall place with both river and forest to protect it. When her people wanted to ward off evil things, they used their own magics, but surely this man who looked like a False-Face was not troubled by such matters. She had seen no other person in all the days she had been in his house.

His days were patterned, and she soon understood their design. When he finished his work for the afternoon, he would cook food again. Then he would talk with her for a while, teaching her new words, making marks with a stick and black stuff to record words she told to him. After that he would go to his sleeping room and she would hear no more until morning came.

She knew she must be patient. Only that would serve her, bringing her to a time when she could leave the tower and find the place in the forest where she had crossed between her world and this one. Surely, if she were clever and quick, she could cross once more into her own homeland. That evening he sat over-long in her room, naming objects, making gestures to explain other matters like actions or ideas. Impatient as she was for him to leave, her long training was her friend. He never suspected she wanted him gone with an intensity that made her forehead ache. By the time he rose at last, yawning, she had added many words to her mental list, and she knew she would remember them. Her mind seldom released anything she learned, useful or not.

When he clumped off to bed, she sighed with relief. Her few possessions were quickly rolled in a cloth he had put there for her use. She was ready to leave as soon as she put her ear to his door and heard his burring breathing, which indicated that he slept.

She hurried down the stair as quietly as a breeze or a bat, her moccasins noiseless on the stone stair that was built into the wall of the tower. Once below, she retrieved her food, secured in an unused room, for she had cut meat from her deer on her last trip to the larder. Adding that to her pack, she unbarred the heavy outer door and pushed it open just enough to let her through, dragging the pack behind her.

When she pushed the door into its frame again, she packed snow at its foot to keep it from opening. Then she hastened down the invisible pathway beside the stream, retracing her steps as nearly as she could, trying to take the exact route she had followed so many days before.

The night was still, frozen into noiselessness. Only the light from the snow guided her steps, for there was no moon, though the sky was clear, for once. Or did this place have a moon, as her own world did? She had never seen one, for the storms had hidden the sky throughout her visit there. No living thing moved in the wood, and except for the quiet crunch of snow beneath her feet, only the occasional slither of snow sliding from branches could be heard. Her own heartbeat was the loudest thing in the forest.

Carefully gauging direction and distance, she came at last to the point where she had seen that unfamiliar oak tree. Leaning against it, she paused and lifted her head, listening, scenting the air, sensing the night and the place. This was the same tree, she was certain, for to one of her upbringing each tree was as individual as a person.

Beyond this point, she had encountered the stream behind her, where no stream existed in her own place. She bore to the right, deeper into the wood. There was a slight indentation in the snow, as if a path ran there beneath the layers, and the bushes were parted as if by the constant passing of men or animals.

She came to another tree, remotely familiar, and she wondered if it was one she had seen only briefly and through swirls of snow. Its shape seemed right, she decided, and she proceeded, going more slowly as she progressed. Her foot sank into the snow for one more step, and there she stopped. For the first time, she sent her orenda among the trees, seeking among the tiny spirits of the sleeping plants. She had stood here before, she knew. Mosses beneath the snow still recalled her passing, though so dimly that only her terrible need would have allowed her to sense that memory.

She stepped forward, one more step. She had not stood in this spot on that other journey. The same kinds of mosses slept beneath the snow, but they retained no impression of her passing feet. Nothing had touched them for a very long while.

Amid the black-on-white silences of the forest, she stood still. It was here that she had come through a doorway from her world into this. That opening was no longer in place, she knew, although a tingle within her orenda told her that some lingering trace of its presence remained.

Two-Moons huddled her bearskin outer robe about her and sat flat in the snow. Perhaps she might summon some dream or vision that could tell her how to re-enter her own place. She drew very deep breaths, relaxing as much as possible and giving herself over to the sender of dream. In time, a picture came clearly before her inner vision. Once more she was borne across a strange nothingness to a village of heavy walls and low, strong-looking houses. Men labored on the walls, building them higher with stones and mud. Other people moved about, some carrying tools or weapons. Women bent over vats of water, scrubbing the kind of clothing Burning-hand wore. All of them seemed to be working without pleasure, as if buried in despair.

A man came into the open space where the women washed and the men toiled. He pushed the other half of the big door through which he had come, and it opened back to show a waiting file of people. The first man stepped backward and swung the long, limp thong in his hand; it cracked viciously, and blood appeared on the face of the first man in line. He fell to his knees and held up his hands, as if pleading.

Two-Moons shook with disgust. What kind of man would lower himself to beg for mercy? Why did he not rise and attack that cruel one with his bare hands?

As the man rose to his feet, she saw with horror that he was bound in some manner to those behind him, linked with unbreakable stuff. One by one the people came forward, all linked by neck and hands and ankles with the shining stuff Burning-hand called metal.

Behind them came other kinds of people, holding weapons in their hands. They cautiously unlinked the captives, keeping watch as if expecting resistance. Leading them forward, one by one, they put a burning red-white stick against their backs, and when it was lifted there was a furious red wound. Each wound was exactly like all the rest, shaped like a spear-point.

"Those are slaves," whispered a voice in her spirit.

"Aireskoi," she breathed, thankful to know that the guide of hunters had not abandoned her in this weird place. Carried upon his spirit, she found herself again at the tower, suspended in the air as if she had climbed a tree to watch. There it was no longer winter but spring. Green filled the forest, and long grasses trailed over the path she had followed.

Burning-hand stood before his doorway, staring down the path, and she turned to see what had made him look so joyful. Then she cried out, though she had no voice in this place. It was her own people who walked that path. She recognized Odatsehe and his mother. Her sisters were there, and even the great Wathadodarho was linked to the rest by neck and hand and foot, like those other slaves had been.

Seven of her tribe, four of them from her own clan, walked up that path, dragging their shackled feet, their heads bowed with shame at being tied so. They bore scars of battle, as well as burns. Then, to her horror, she saw that those were like the marks she had seen burned into the flesh of the slaves in her vision. That had been of a place, she now realized, in the same valley where she had seen Burning-hand disappear. The valley with two moons in its sky. Something changed....

...And she opened her eyes. Snow and stillness surrounded her, yet she felt as if she were surrounded by enemies whom she must overcome, in order to save her people. She rose and took up her pack. As if pursued, she fled back to the tower and slipped into the door, barring it behind her.

She listened at Burning-hand's door as she came to the landing, but his snores reassured her. He had slept and knew nothing of her going. Then she went into her own chamber and closed the door. There were still warm coals in the fireplace; she blew them into a blaze, adding fuel from the pile she kept beside the fire-hole. Then she curled into her robes, on the floor before the fire, and closed her eyes, thinking about what she had seen. Burning-hand wanted her people—or some of her people. She had no idea what his intentions might be, but the memory of those burn marks, those shackles, told her that it was for no good purpose. She must watch him, learn all she could about his arts and his needs, in order to prevent this thing from happening.

"Aireskoi," she murmured. "Taonhiawagi! Help me to preserve my people from this evil man. Help me to keep them walking in freedom in our own forests, upon our own mountain. Help me, Taonhiawagi, Aireskoi. Help me!"

Smoke curled around her as wind came down the chimney. It touched her face and the dark fur of her beaver skin robe like a caress. Then it was gone, and Two-Moons-in-the-Sky slept.

# CHAPTER ELEVEN

## LET SPARKS FLY FREE

Every morning for a century Lallius had risen sluggishly, shuddering at the damp chill of his tower. Even after so long, he still missed the dry warmth of his native land, the scents of familiar growing things in the fields and meadows, even the stinks of the city. The weather of this place was terrible. Now even for his kind he was growing old. His bones protested more every year, when he forced them to move from his bed. It was time he had help, although this woman never offered or consented to that.

Even so, it was a bit more bearable to have someone to share his isolation. Though this woman was not the witless primitive he had expected, filled with raw and untutored talents that he had thought to use for his own purposes, she was, perhaps, more interesting because of those qualities. He could not solve the puzzle—why did she deny she was a woman and claim to be a warrior? Here, as in his own world, women were slaves or toys or concubines, unless they were of royal blood; those were skilled politicians, able to manipulate others for their own purposes. No woman he had ever known or heard about knew how to use weapons or would have touched them if she had. Women did not hunt, being content to allow their men to do the difficult and dangerous tasks.

This woman asked nothing of him except to be left to

her own devices. When her supply of meat ran low, she did not use his game in the larder, which he drew into his snares with simple spells, but took her bow and disappeared into the forest. Even in winter, amid such snows, she always returned with something, a hare or a deer or even a wild pig.

She gathered her own wood for her fire, though she never brought any from the forest for him. She did not appear to know, far less to accept, that a woman was only made for the use of a man. With her, it was obvious this might not be as true as he had thought it to be. This intrigued him strangely, and more than once he had been tempted to go to her chamber and make use of her in the way he knew best. However, something made him think long before doing that and to hesitate once he had thought.

Her hard brown hands held her knife with complete confidence. They aimed her bow steadily and her arrows flew straight to her targets. Her slender back was straight beneath the weight of even the heaviest carcass. She was no soft and pliant victim, like those who littered his past. She promised pain to anyone who tried to dominate her, and Lallius, so apt at giving pain to others, recognized that. He did not like to suffer it himself.

On this morning he rose, grumpy and out of sorts, and heated thin soup in one of his vessels over an alcohol burner. The alembic was not truly appropriate for cookery, but he was not a meticulous person. He had learned long since that leftover soup in his vessel did little to alter the result of an experiment.

When he finished his scanty meal, he went out onto the landing and stared at the woman's door. He smelled no hint of cookery, but that did not disturb him; he had learned early that she ate only once each day, and then sparingly. He moved to the door and tapped on the old wood with a knuckle. For a moment there was no reply, but then the door opened and she stood looking through the narrow crack she had allowed. She was there in body, but he saw at once that her spirit had withdrawn from him.

When he looked into her eyes, he knew the tentative communication that had been growing between them had ended, as if she turned her thoughts away from the things he was teaching her. What had happened in the night to change her so? The evening had been, as far as he could tell, quite friendly and cooperative. He had felt no friction, and he had made no demands upon her.

Now, feeling uncertain, he pretended to see no difference in her attitude. "Good day, Mistress. It seems to be a better day than those that have gone before. Perhaps we may proceed with our lessons this morning."

Her gaze was withering, and a string of heathenish syllables came from her lips, only a few of which he knew. Yet there was one, repeated more than once, about which he had made notes. Aksen. It had referred to one of the more outré pictures in one of his books. He must look at his notes....

Lallius turned, his thoughts elsewhere, and went into his own rooms, though he felt her stare against his back as he moved across the landing. Locating his folio, he turned the stiff pages until he came to his freshest writing. Yes— aksen, plainly transcribed, with the notes beneath it.

"This seems to denote wickedness or evil, illness, or perhaps ugliness. The woman said this repeatedly while tapping on the picture of a gargoyle devouring a child. This was a drawing Master Albertus made especially for the book she was examining. Aksen seems to be a strongly denunciatory word in her language."

So, she had called him evil, face to face, eye to eye. She was correct, of course, but he had not expected her to realize that so soon and without any overt indication on his part. How had she, in the space of a single night, come to understand him so well? He pondered the question all through that day. He did not approach her door again, but wandered about the cold tower for a while before going out into the bright and icy day. Beyond the outer door he found a disturbance in the snow where the crust was broken by footprints. Even to his unskilled eye, it was clear that she had gone out, closing the door behind her.

Her tracks had indented the crust beyond that spot, and he could follow them without effort. She had gone down the path, along the stream, toward the place from which she had come. Had she been seeking his doorway? And if so, how had she reacted when she found no trace of it?

He was not shod for walking through snow, but he kept on, nevertheless, following the stream to the game trail that led into the forest. There he found a great tree, where, according to her tracks, she had paused for some time. Past that, she had moved forward along the trail to a spot in the midst of a small clearing. What had she done there?

He studied the marks in the snow. Surely she had sat here for some time, for he found animal hairs like those from her crude fur cloak frozen into the snow. The warmth of her body had melted out a small depression, and when she left it had frozen again.

At that point, without going any farther, she had turned back to return to the tower. Why?

He stared around him at the black lace of leafless branches, the motionless boles of the trees, standing like dark columns against the stark white background. Nothing told him what he must learn.

What had she done here? What had she seen, alone in the frozen wood in the middle of the night? He could see no sign that she had attempted to summon demons, as he did. No Pentagram marked the snow, and it was known to all sorcerers that this was the only thing that could protect them from the arcane powers possessed by those they summoned.

He could find no trace of any symbol at all. He stared

at the mark where she had sat; then, shrugging, he turned back toward the tower. What power did that woman command? On the first night she had resisted his attempts to shake her from her hiding place. Why had he forgotten that? It was no easy thing to do, and in no way could her resistance be accidental. As he trudged along, his feet half frozen, he pondered this riddle.

Except for his original trap, set in her own place, nothing he had done had affected her. It seemed as if she were in some way immune to the kind of power he had always thought to be limitless. How could that be? Those he had known in his own world and in this one had agreed that those were irresistible potencies, though in this world they were linked with evil things, and in his own they had been considered mere tools.

How had this woman's life and person been different, making her capable of standing apart, untouched by his Arcana?

Lallius approached his door, which was weathered and worn, and through which he had gone and come for almost a century. Through it he had dragged an occasional forester or woodcutter or child straying from its home, but it had been very long since any human being had passed this way. His depredations among those following the river had warned them away, but it was most inconvenient.

To perform the Major Arcana one needed human sacrifice. It had been too long since he had been able to practice the most important of his arts. But now—he grinned, his face almost cracking with the cold—now there was a warm human body within the tower. The body of a woman. First there would be pleasure, and then pain and terror. That was the strong meat of life. Why had he waited so long to make her serve her only legitimate purpose?

Heaving the door open, he slipped through and secured it. Taking from a high shelf a heavy lock whose wrought iron key lay beside it, he slid the tang through the iron hasps on door and frame and turned the key in the cobwebby keyhole. It snapped shut with a rusty clank. She could not leave by this route, and he would give her no warning that their relationship had changed. She would not know soon enough to leave by way of her window. By the time she understood his intentions, it would be entirely too late for her to save herself.

He stood in the stairwell and held up a stiff hand. Concentrating upon his own fingers, he made them begin to glow. Sparks of cold light formed about each fingertip, and by the light of his own hand he climbed the stair. As he moved, he shook with silent laughter. Once on the landing he stood before her door, quiet as the draught that lived in the tower, and shook his burning hand. Sparks flew about him like disturbed moths. He laid his hand against the old panel of her door. The cold fire that lived within it marked a dark print against the wood. Then, still laughing silently, he went into his own rooms and closed his own door. Now there would be time for him to rest.

# CHAPTER TWELVE

## The Watcher in the Sweat-House

The long ordeal of purification was shortened a bit because Runs-Bucks had already been fasting for days. There was no need for that, though there was still much the shamans must say to him. Rituals remained to be performed, chants made, and songs sung. Four times he went into the sweat-lodge to be cleansed in its steams. Three times he came out feeling faint and thin as winter sunlight. When he entered for the fourth time, he wondered in his heart if the sweat ceremony would leave him strength enough to accomplish his task.

The stones were red-hot, and the gourds of water that he poured onto them filled the tiny bark house with mist which rose into his face, filled his lungs. Runs-Bucks felt himself fainting, and yet he now held the talisman, secured in a tight pouch so the steam would not reach its contents. When he reached to finger it, that touch steadied him.

He sat on a rock amid the steam, feeling his orenda growing stronger, even as his flesh weakened. His eyes closed without his willing them to, and he slipped into a strange, dreamlike state. Once more he was outside his body, moving through an unfamiliar forest.

Once again that tower loomed ahead of him, but this time he was compelled to approach its door. To his astonishment, he moved through the heavy wood as easily as if it had been smoke. Then he was inside the place, which was hollow and very tall and made of stone. He drifted upward, as smoke moves into the sky, until he hung at the top of the stone steps. Something powerful pulled him through a door there; once inside the room he hovered in his misty state, watching the terrible man who was there.

He was tall and thin, standing naked within a pattern marked onto the floor. Tiny torches, no larger than Runs-Bucks's finger, stood at each angle of that pattern, burning with smoke and stench, though Runs-Bucks could not quite know how he perceived that, for his nose was very far away.

The man spoke, his words faint and incomprehensible murmurs, seeming to come from a great distance. The candle flames wavered, as if a draught moved them, though the door was still tightly closed. Runs-Bucks felt a chill, even in this not-body he inhabited, and he knew his hand must be clutching the talisman, back there in the sweat-lodge. Something had entered the room, though he could see nothing. The man did, it was clear, for he focused his gaze upon a spot outside the pattern surrounding him. He spoke to it, and from the spot to which he spoke there came a cold that made frost form on the stone walls and twinkle in the candle light.

Runs-Bucks felt a vibration, which he could sense only by the quiver of water in a cup on the table and the faint disturbance of the smoke from the candles. Whatever had come into the room was real, he knew, visible or not.

Once the disturbance eased, the man stiffened, still within his pattern, and began turning deliberately, staring at each part of the room as it came into his field of vision. Those colorless eyes swept over the spot where Runs-Bucks hung. The warrior felt that cold glance as it passed over him, and he shuddered.

The man did not change his expression, and he did not slow in his turning. Runs-Bucks knew himself to be invisible to the strange one, and probably also to whatever being had answered his summons. Even in his disembodied condition, Runs-Bucks felt an unease that evidently permeated the room and touched the white-faced man in its center.

As the man completed his scan, the flames burned lower. He paused, facing as before, and spoke again to the spot from which the disturbance had come. The candle smoke thinned, and something went from the room, still invisible.

The thin man drooped, as if wearied by his task, and slowly stepped from his pattern. A black robe hung from a hook, and the man draped it loosely about him. He stared again around the room, but this time he did not seek for something unseen. It seemed he looked for comfort or reassurance.

A container of dark liquid sat beside the cup Runs-Bucks had observed. The black robed man emptied the water from the cup and poured into it some of the liquid. As it moved, it steamed, and once it was inside the cup it boiled gently for a moment. Grim-faced, the wizard looked down at it. Then he lifted the cup and tossed its contents down his throat. Something about that action alerted Runs-Bucks. Within his spirit, he spoke to Taonhiawagi. "My spirit stands here, without body, without hands. Stand beside it, Taonhiawagi, though this is a place where you may never have come before.

"Help me to understand, Master of Life. Give me the wisdom to do what is needed, for I sense evil in this man. There is wicked purpose here, and I feel it must threaten even our own people. Lend me your strength, if you have strength in this strange world."

The man interrupted his prayer, for he moved toward the door, holding the robe closely about him as if he were cold, carrying the cup. Runs-Bucks slid through the wood even as it began to open, and he watched as the other man went across the way to another door and touched it lightly.

The white-face's free hand rose to shoulder height and began to glow, each finger a separate torch, even as Runs-Bucks had seen his own hand glow when he touched that warped stone face which was now within the talisman. As the pale man's hand touched the door, Runs-Bucks was reaching back toward his own distant flesh, willing his own hand to grasp the talisman even more tightly. And it did—he could feel it, even at so great a distance. He flowed back into the tower with renewed strength and watched as the door swung open beneath that burning touch.

Two-Moons was beyond that door. He felt it now, with no sense he had ever possessed before but with complete certainty. She breathed—indeed, she was sleeping—within that room into which this alien being was moving. Although he had no time to think it, Runs-Bucks found himself inside the room as well. Now he hung, invisible, in the air between the door and the sleeping-skins upon which Two-Moons lay.

The man with the burning hand was white-faced, and his features were lined with cruel and terrible creases. He looked at the sleeping woman, a grimace warping his expression, which was revealed by the small fire Two-Moons had left burning in the fire-hole.

Many times Runs-Bucks had seen that look when the Onondaga had raided the villages of other tribes or those tribes had raided them. It was the look of a man intent upon cruel acts. Suddenly, Runs-Bucks found himself warm. Though he had no body, whatever he was at that moment was pulsing with hot anger, which he knew was not his own. He had no knowledge of what might be causing this, but he knew he was being moved by the will of Taonhiawagi.

"Taonhiawagi," he said within himself, and there was a presence beside him in that tower in this alien land. The

Master of Life had not lost sight of this most distant of his children.

The black-robed man, however, seemed unaware that someone stood between him and his prey. He held that glowing hand high, and sparks flew from it toward the furred cloak that covered Two-Moons as she slept. With great deliberateness, those sparks flew, and Runs-Bucks sensed, without understanding how, that some power within them was directed against the woman in the bed.

He was suddenly, without thinking about it, between those sparks and their goal. He opened his spirit wide on the air, holding all that he was as a shield between this woman who was a part of him and the man who behaved as if he were one with the False Face and every other evil thing.

The sparks came to a halt where he hung, gathering in motionless sparkles as if caught in a spider web. Frozen fireflies, they hung against the barrier he had imposed across their path, and the man who sent them uttered a shocked gasp. His eyes, deep and strange in his white face, glared about as he tried to see some reason for the failure of his attempt. Evidently he saw nothing, felt nothing, though Runs-Bucks was there, thwarting him.

"Taonhiawagi," said Runs-Bucks, "let me slay him!"

"This is not one of mine, child of the Onondaga. Even I cannot slay him, for he belongs to other powers than my own," came the whispered thought in Runs-Bucks's mind. "Yet I will not allow him to slay those who are mine. His powers—and they are very real and strong and dangerous—are not those I know, as he is not of a world we know.

"He calls upon beings like to me and yet very different. I can feel them gathered about him, throbbing in the air and in the stone, but I cannot see them. They cannot, I am convinced, see me—or you, even though the dimensions in which they exist must be like to my own."

Knowing nothing about dimensions, Runs-Bucks was puzzled by that reply. The lands of the Onondaga, the Kanonsionni, the legends of distant forebears who had come from the east over the great water, those things bounded his life. Still, one thing was clear to him.

"Are those other spirits your kindred?" he asked.

The answering thought was disturbed. "No! Not in any sense. Child of the Mountain, you will find it hard to understand my thought, for we are not in any place connected by land or by water with that in which you and Two-Moons were born. Though this place is on the same world, not only great distances but long spans of time divide it from the lands you know.

"Only the cruel misuse of power brought Two-Moons here, and only through the use of power were you able to send your thought here to find her. The spirits who rule this place are like and unlike those who rule the forests of the Onondaga. We may be, remotely, of the same kind, but more than time and distance divide us. In my world even the most mischievous spirits respect life and those who hold life. Here that is not true."

At that moment the tall man moved forward cautiously, holding the burning hand before him as if it were a shield. When he came to the barrier where the sparks waited he found no hindrance to his own passage. He walked through it without learning what might hold his sparks fast in mid-air. He paused there and looked with something like dread at the sleeping woman. "She is strong," he said aloud, and something translated his words into Runs-Bucks' invisible ear. "But she is, after all, small and only a woman. I am a man and I can overcome her. And, as well, she sleeps...." The man set the now empty cup on a table beside the wall, flung aside his cloak and, naked, approached the sleeping place.

Anger pulsed through Runs-Bucks, burning brighter than any flame. With all his strength of will, the warrior cried to Two-Moons' sleeping spirit, "Awake! Danger! Wake, Two-Moons, and defend yourself!"

Her black eyes opened, to recognize the naked white shape of Burning-hand looming over her. She moved, and Runs-Bucks could see shock in her face, then anger, and then determination. With one smooth motion, she slipped off the bed-pile on the other side, standing only long enough to snatch her flint knife from the bearskin. Then she was free of that narrow space, in the wider area before the dying fire. There she waited, and the tall man leaped upon her.

Filled with anger and frustration, Runs-Bucks was completely helpless to aid her. In this dimension he had no body, and only the long years of communication and affection between them had allowed him to wake her in time. Now she must battle alone, while Runs-Bucks waited, his spirit in agony.

There came a gasp of pain as the woman kicked for the groin, and the man ended his leap in a heap on the floor at Two-Moons' feet. She darted across the room to gather her heavy cloak, her weapons, and a small pack, lying ready as if for travel. She dropped them beside the doorway as her opponent rose and rushed her again.

This time she ducked beneath his widespread arms and swayed to one side. As he passed her she scored his side deeply with her flint blade. He flinched backward, and she kicked one knee from beneath him, sending him down again. This time she kicked him in the head, the impact of her moccasin thumping his skull against the hard floor of the chamber.

She stood waiting as he sat up slowly and stared down at the ooze of blood from his side. When he looked up, her eyes were cold and hostile. "Do not approach me again," she said, and though she spoke in her own tongue, he seemed to understand.

When she tried the door, it was secured in some way

she seemed to understand. Still helpless to aid her, Runs-Bucks saw her swing open the panel and slip through, carrying her bundle. Glancing back, she frowned as if puzzled by something she could not quite understand. Then, with a slow nod, she moved back into the room, to the table that held the cup from which the man had drunk earlier. She sniffed the thing, eyed the container doubtfully, and smashed it against the stone wall. Then she went out of the room and the door closed behind her. The watcher could hear a fumbling beyond it, as if she were securing it to keep the white-faced man inside the chamber.

Runs-Bucks would have sighed, had he been inside his own flesh. He watched the man rise slowly to his feet and dab at the bleeding wound with the tail of his cloak. He stared around him as if dazed by the swift sequence of events that took place there. Then he moved toward the door, which he evidently could not unlatch but touched with the hand that had glowed so brightly before.

Now its glow was damped to a glimmer, but whatever powered it was not enough to make the panel swing open to let him through. Runs-Bucks did not wait, but wafted through the door and stared out into the snowy evening.

Two-Moons was well down the stairway inside the tower, moving with ease as she went. Reassured, he paused to think and found himself chilled in some non-physical manner he had never known. He hung in a thick mist, but trees flickered past....

He opened his eyes to see the interior of the sweat-lodge, the wisps of steam from the rocks, still rosy with heat. About his neck the talisman hung heavy, and he found that his hands were clenched so hard about it that it took great effort to loose them.

He stood and stretched, feeling as if he had sat there for days instead of the relatively short time it must have been for the stones to hold heat still. Folding back the door-hide, he moved, naked, out into the snow. The shamans stood there, waiting, and their faces showed surprise that he had emerged so soon.

Runs-Bucks held up the talisman. "This took my spirit through to that other world," he said. "I saw our brother Two-Moons. There is danger for her there, as well as for all of us. Something is there that we have never known, and even Taonhiawagi cannot destroy it."

There was a stunned silence as he walked through the snow, his skin steaming lightly with inner heat, toward the longhouse. Behind him came the elders, silent and bewildered at this unexpected turn of events.

# CHAPTER THIRTEEN

## IN THE FOREST

Two-Moons moved swiftly once she had left the chamber. She had locked Burning-hand into the room, but she also wanted to leave the tower secured against him, if he should imitate her climb down the tower. Gathering her possessions, checking her weapons, and wrapping herself in the warm cloak, she went into one of the lower chambers on the other side of the tower, and went out through the window into the snow, a much shorter climb than she had made earlier.

Once outside, she turned toward the river and moved toward the opposite shore from the one she knew. Not again would she sit in that tiny hut and wait for Burning-hand to reveal his purpose. Within the last few minutes she had learned all she needed to know of him.

She followed the track she had made in the snow when she went to find fuel for her fire in the log-jam there. A pile of deadfall had dammed that side of the stream, forming a bridge between island and shore. Its tangle did not hold snow, and she stepped into it, setting her moccasins onto branches and logs that would not show any mark. She climbed over the obstacle quickly, and she felt that Burning-hand was too little of a woodsman to recognize any except the most obvious track. It would have required

Onondaga eyes to see the slight disturbances among the riffles of snow lying along random branches.

The forest beyond the stream was thicker and wilder than the one she had seen before. No track of man or game marked a trail through the thick bushes. Only the wide-branching arms of the great oaks and beeches, still holding a few dead leaves, kept the forest floor clear of low growth, once she had moved through the tangle along the edge of the stream. In that ancient forest it was silent and still. The night was now dark, but snow-light guided her as she picked her way along the least drifted ways, dragging her cloak behind her to muddle any track. Though the cold struck through her buckskin shirt, under-cloak of beaver, and leggings, she ignored it, moving warily.

She watched closely for shadows that might reveal a stump hole or burrow, for a broken ankle or leg would doom her to die in the snow. She would never call out for help, knowing that Burning-hand was the only one who could hear her call and come to find her helpless. Once she was well into the forest, she wrapped herself again in the robe and hitched her bow so that it was covered but still near to hand. This forest, as she had learned over the time of her captivity, held game for the taking. Her bow would feed her for as long as necessary.

How long might that be? She was thinking about that as she moved through the wood. As well, she was wondering what had awakened her, just in time to halt Burning-hand's assault upon her. Something had called to her, though she could not remember hearing any sound. A shout had rung inside her heart and called her from sleep. Impossible though it was, she felt in her spirit that it had been Runs-Bucks who shouted to warn her.

She walked a very long way, and the sky above the oak branches was paling with dawn when she halted. This was a place where she might camp in safety, she thought, a tree so old and stooped it seemed to be holding itself up with crutches, for the branches of its lower third swept the ground in a great arc. They still bore a rustling roof of leaves, dried on the twigs, which held away much of the snow. When she stooped and went into that shelter, she found that the trunk was like a wall, solidly bulking to the north, a bulwark against the wind. There was also a fire-pit between a pair of gnarled roots, thrusting waist-high from the base of the trunk to grip the ground in thick fingers.

Two-Moons grunted. Someone had lined that pit with stones, placing shelving slabs over its top to focus the heat and to hide the light. It was a good place to warm yourself or to cook without calling the attention of anyone abroad in the wood. She wondered what hunter had made this his camp—she had never heard the word outlaw and would not have understood the concept.

Beneath the leaning trunk and thick branches she found it relatively dry, with layered leaves under light snow whose bottom-most layers were dry enough for starting a fire. In her pouch, as always, she carried her fire sticks, and though it was not easy to kindle a blaze in snow, she managed it at last.

Her fingers ached before the twirling hardwood stick raised a thin thread of smoke in the hole in the softwood, but once she added tinder, she soon had a glowing coal to set carefully amid dry leaves. Soon she had a vigorous blaze burning in that convenient fire-pit.

She had not truly rested for two nights. Now she must sleep in order to hunt tomorrow. With no food at hand, other than the strips of meat she had taken from her store, and unwilling to return to the tower for any reason, she knew her bow must feed her. Strength and warmth depended upon a well nourished body, when one was forced to live outdoors in winter, and she was determined to survive here on her own.

She climbed onto a low, flat limb that lay along the ground beside the ash-banked fire pit. Wrapping the bearskin snugly from head to foot, she slept well, and when she woke there was a glimmer of sun touching the frost-tipped treetops. Lying on the branch, she stared up through the layers of limbs, judging this to be a very tall tree, despite its hunched shape. Possibly it would be tall enough to give her a look at the forest lying about it, which would be helpful as she planned her hunt. She secured her moccasins with thongs and began to climb, finding good finger and toeholds in the grooved bark. There were a few rotted branches, but she never trusted her weight to one, when she reached that level, and made her way safely to the top.

From that point she could see for a long distance across the forest, although there were tops of great trees that interrupted her view. Turning slowly, keeping her feet and hands braced, she looked back toward the river and the tower. It was now only a thick splinter of black rising from the icing of snow covering its island.

She had come a long way. Burning-hand was not woodsman enough to follow her, she was certain, for he obviously knew nothing of woodcraft. Here she might be safe from him for as long as she chose to remain.

Climbing down again, she built the fire up solidly, after uncovering the deep layer of red coals. She knew she must hunt for meat, for she had used a lot of energy in her flight from the tower, and that must be replenished.

The call she had heard, warning her to wake, had come from one of her own people, she became more and more sure. Runs-Bucks was not idle—he would come, if it were possible at all. She had only to survive here, waiting and keeping her spirit ready to answer any further call.

"Aireskoi," she breathed, but there was no answering touch within her orenda. The guide and guardian of hunters was busy among her own people, she knew, and she could not expect him to remain with her when she had no immediate need. She hid her possessions high in the tree, secured on the upper sides of big branches that would hide them from anyone below. While she worked she thought of the events of the night before. Burning-hand had come in the night, and not to teach her words. He must have known, from her cold greeting of the morning, that she had come to understand his purpose with regard to her people.

Though he had given no sign of that, he was devious, as she knew too well. He had come to use her body and to force her to work his will after he subdued her. The thought made her shiver with fury. Was there no honor among his kind? Did they pretend friendship and then betray the trust they created? The Onondaga had many enemies, but once the League of the Longhouse, the Kanonsionni, was formed, all the tribes linked by a common tongue lived in peace in their own places.

If one had a quarrel with another, there was no pretense at friendship until the matter was settled by the Kanonsionni. Only in extreme cases had there been war within the League in her lifetime. Only when the Algonkians came did her people take up their weapons for battle. Burning-hand did not live like anyone of whom she had ever heard tales told. Alone, without wife or child or friend to tell jokes with about the campfire, he seemed cold and remote, inhuman. What kind was he, and were all those here like him? Or did he bring that alien way with him from the world with two moons from which she had seen him snatched?

When she was finished with her tasks, she took up her bow and left the shelter of the tree. She did that with great care, making certain she left no recognizable track. She had covered the fire-pit with ashes and dirt to save the coals without betraying the fact, in case she must remain here for long.

For the first time since her escape, she opened her senses to the air, seeking to mesh her own orenda with that of this alien forest. There was compatibility, she found.

The trees and the dormant plants drowsed in their winter states, but there was no enmity toward any who walked through the wood. Many small lives hid in deep burrows and in the hollows of trees. Other, greater lives could be felt also, and she took care not to trouble them. If she attracted the attention of one of the wild boars here, she would be forced to freeze in some treetop, and in this weather she could not survive there for long.

As she neared her tree she felt a quiver in the linkage of orenda. Pausing in a thicket bordering one side of the tree's self-created clearing, she focused her sensing. Men had passed here recently. Two of them at least.

Two-Moons wrapped her kill and her roots in her under-cloak and hid it amid thick bushes. Taking her bow and nocking an arrow, she slipped to the right, remaining in cover and circling the shelter-tree. Halfway around, she sank to her knees, hearing voices.

"Someone's been nigh here, Athol," said one. "Ye canna deny the stone's hot and there be marks where summat's walked beneath the tree. I am not fool enow to say who it might be, but I'll wager it's not that white-faced devil from the tower."

Two-Moons had learned a great deal of his language from Burning-hand in the weeks of their lessons. She now understood something of the gist of what was said, and she listened intently as the other man spoke.

"True," said the other voice. "He is not made of the stuff of foresters, though I'd like to make trial to see of what stuff he may actually be. One day I will do that and use his guts for garters." His voice was more assured, deeper than the other, yet it held an edge that went through Two-Moons like a blade. This was a dangerous man, far more dangerous than Burning-hand could ever have been without using magics.

The first man grumbled under his breath, and now she could see him as he moved into position beyond the drooping branches. He was kicking about beneath the tree, and he seemed to be re-kindling the fire. That was inconvenient. She had food hidden in the bushes, and her thick under-cloak, but she had no desire to find another place to build fire, or to leave her fur cloak secured in the branches. It was too bulky to wear for hunting, but now she wished she had taken it with her. Without it, she might awake in the morning with frozen feet.

The shorter man came to the edge of the shelter and peered out at the ice-tinted sky, which was now clouding over. The sun was gone, and more snow might well fall before night.

"Garh!" he growled. "Weather fit for nothing! My Grandsire tells me that before yon demon wizard came to the tower the winters were milder than now, and men could hunt these woods without fear. The Lord at the time heard the cries of the poor, unlike Ulric, curse his bones!"

"No talk of Ulric," the other commanded. "He will feel the weight of my hand soon enough, but until he returns to his keep that must wait. Now I look to that black tower and my interest is keen. Many have disappeared nearby through the years, you say?"

"For the past hundred-year, Athol Bladingford, men and women and children have gone missing who ventured up the river from Keely Village. Cattleherds and washerwomen, foresters and huntsmen, children berrying or tickling for fish in the stream have gone and been heard of no more. Why, think you, does that goodly village stand empty, its stout cottages losing their thatch to the wind, the stone inn holding nothing but bats? Our grandsires were no fools, and they knew soon enough that their new neighbor was a danger to them. Yet the Lord could do nothing, for the island is freehold, and its owner at the time was no less than one Michael Scot, the wizard.

"No one dared trouble him, either in his own northern country or hereabouts, for it was unwise to cross him.

Deaths and sicknesses plagued those who tried. His tenant could not be troubled, either, though the demon had no such scruple about troubling others. The Lord moved the boundaries of the village to the place where it has stood for eighty-seven years, and the people were safe—or safer—than they were." The older man spat out into the snow. Two-Moons was lost amid an unfamiliar torrent of words, yet their sense came through to her. So Burning-hand had troubled those who belonged here, it was clear. The information might be useful, one day.

"Michael Scot...." the voice was thoughtful. "Now there's a name out of the dark past. Sorcerer, correct? Necromancer, I have no doubt, and other unsavory things. I have often wondered if it was not the tales of the credulous that brought him down at last."

"He gave us no trouble, indeed," the gravelly voice said. "Nor did the little foreigner, my Grandsire said. But yon black skeleton came at last, and then the bad times began in earnest."

"But if the village was moved eighty-seven years ago—surely the wizard had a son. Surely it cannot be the same man living there."

"It is the same, believe me or no. He has looked the same, been the same through three generations of my family. Some who dared have spied upon him, betimes, and their descriptions tally.

"No woman has ever entered that tower willingly, and those dragged in have never walked out again. Nor has any man or child. Long ago we set watchers along the path between tower and village, that none might unknowingly stray toward it. Now we lose no more to him, and it has come to my mind to wonder if he hungers."

Two-Moons shuddered, remembering the look on that pale-eyed face staring down at her in the night. He did indeed hunger, and for no nourishment normal bellies might welcome. Once more she saw in her mind the shackled figures in that valley of two moons. She could see those marks upon the bodies of her own clan and tribe who walked in her vision. What else did Burning-hand do? Was slavery the worst of his faults? If these men were his enemies, might they be her friends? Something chilled inside her. No, they were aliens and strangers. Their voices held not only anger but a careless cruelty that she found unsettling. To them, as to Burning-hand, she would be only a woman to use, and she could not risk that.

Still, she needed her furry cloak and the other things in her pack in the tree. Might she frighten them away? An arrow from nowhere was a startling thing, she knew from experience. Silent, braced amid the bushes, she drew her bow. The arrow whisked past her cheek, and there came a solid thunk as it buried itself in the trunk of the oak. She had placed it neatly between two limbs, almost directly between the two heads now facing each other above the fire-pit.

That taught her something valuable. These two were warriors. They were down instantly between the bastion-like roots, and there was no incautious peering over to see who had sent this arrow their way. Given that reaction, it was probable that one or the other was snaking around the far end of the root to go into the bushes behind the tree in order to take her from the rear.

Quietly she backed into the thicket and out the other side into a clear area beneath another big tree. She edged around it, avoiding the unmarked snow until she reached the clear space beneath the biggest of the trees and sank into a tangle of vines where snow had fallen from the branches above in a rough tumble. Let them hunt. She had been hunted before by Lenni Lenape, who had no equals as huntsmen.

The tree trunk was at her back. There was room to draw her bow without moving anything to betray her presence. One who came into her line of fire would find himself skewered like a woodchuck, yet she found it in her to regret killing either. If they were here to harry Burninghand, that could only be to her advantage. She must avoid killing them if she could.

They were not clumsy—only an occasional swish or muted crackle told her they moved through the wood. One went east, the other west, and she knew they had assessed the angle of the arrow in the tree between then. They knew she must be to the south, and would attempt to trap her between them. If she were stupid enough to move they might succeed, but she had no intention of stirring from her hidden nook. She listened to them as they crept and listened and crept again until the light was almost gone from the sky. At last they spoke again, and she knew they must have met amid the bushes where she hid first.

"He's gone, Athol. There be no sign of a track in the clearing, and that was too long a shot to come from beyond this thicket. He must have been lying there all the time, listening to us as we talked."

"Think you it was the sorcerer?" Athol asked.

There came a snort of disgust. "That one would not know one end of an arrow from the other, and this, look ye, is unlike any arrow I have seen. See the shaft? Not the ash we use hereabout. And the fletching? A kind of feather I've never found in all my life. The style is new to me, and this arrow gives me a strange feeling in the gut. I mislike this altogether."

"If not Lallius, then who?" The other voice was impatient.

"There be others outlawed besides yourself, Athol Bladeford. There be others than I who hunt these forests, and none are men I'd choose to meet by night. We'd best go back to my hut and come at yon tower from another direction." Though she understood little of the last exchange, Two-Moons followed their progress as they worked their way back north and east. This suited her

116

well—with more than one enemy at hand, perhaps Burn-ing-hand would be distracted. When the call came for which she waited, then she could answer it.

And then there would be a reckoning!

# CHAPTER FOURTEEN

## CONJURATION

Lallius delayed for a very long while before he could bring himself to leave this room by way of the window, but in no other way could he escape. For some time he thought the woman would not dare to leave him penned so and would return to free him. She could not conquer the lock he had placed on the tower door, he was certain. Then he had a sickening thought. The tower held other windows than this. If she could not open the door, she might well venture out, as she had done before. She had done that in the darkness—surely it would be easier by day.

He was bruised and battered from flinging himself against the door, but his doors had been meant to hold against prisoners within or attackers without. The outer bolts were of thick black iron, let into sockets in the stone of the walls. The wood was oak, as thick as his arm; no human muscle could split them without the aid of a ram or an axe.

He knew he must try the dizzy way down the tower wall, and it made him reel to think of it. Even to look out of the unshuttered window made him cringe; a thirty-foot drop lay below it. Worse than all, he was naked. He could not get to his own room to find garments to shield him from the cold. He gnawed his knuckles with frustration and wondered why he had risked attacking this unwilling and dangerous woman. Something inside him had sensed that she was guarded by other powers than those he knew.

Luckily, the thin cloak he had tossed aside lay on the floor. It was poor protection, but there was nothing better at hand except the awkward covers of the bed. He dared not risk entangling himself during such a terrible descent. Wrapping the black fabric about him, he tied it about his waist with a strip ripped from the hem and, with his teeth, tore holes to free his arms.

Leaning out as far as possible, he tried to see the window of his bedroom, only a few yards away, but around the curve of the wall. A glimpse of the frame, the edge of a shutter was all he could see. He knew he had not fastened the shutters well, for they had rattled in the wind all evening. If he could sidle around the sheer wall to that window, he might be able to open the shutter and gain the sanctuary of his own chambers. The fall would be no more perilous attempting that than trying the downward climb. Nothing was to be gained by waiting.

He crawled awkwardly onto the window ledge and pushed the shutter back against the wall. The stone course just below the sill offered a narrow edge, which showed clearly in the weak sunlight. Twisting himself around, he felt with his freezing toes for purchase on the icy stone. The thing was horribly narrow, and he had to set his foot along it lengthwise, and even then half his foot hung over space. His other foot found a crack, and he caught the edge of the shutter in a desperate grip and edged along, a few inches at a time.

Once he moved past the shutter, he had to work his fingers into the crevices between the stones that formed the wall. It was dizzy work. He found himself growing sick as he moved along, but he gained his own window after what seemed a very long while and hooked his right-hand fingers beneath the shutter. Even as he jerked at the wood, he realized it was foolish. The leaf swung back against him and wiped him off the wall, to fall in a flutter of black cloth, flailing his blue-white arms and legs as he went backward into a snowdrift.

He lay for a moment, blinking up through the snow at a drift of ice-bright cloud. He felt himself as he rose, and found that he seemed undamaged. As he got to his feet, he felt no more pain than he had felt before. Some one of his dark powers must have been with him, he thought.

However, he was now outside the tower, all but naked, and everything he owned was inside the structure. He stalked on rapidly numbing feet to the door and shook it hard. The iron-banded oak didn't move. Only his flesh and bones vibrated with the effort.

Damn that lock! Why had it failed to keep her inside? It looked as if it would keep him out with complete efficiency. Rage surged through him, warming him somewhat. Why had he locked that door? Why had he not opened the shutter on the other side of his own window? Why?

Then something very quiet spoke from deep inside him. "Why did you not control your lust? Lacking that control, why did you not sit in that room in which the woman left you? There was fire there, and a bit of meat left from her meal. You could have conjured a helper to open the bolt from outside. Did you forget that you are an adept? A sorcerer—holding the skills of two worlds! Lallius, you have been a fool."

He realized that he had been. Instead of using his great powers to free himself, he had lost his control in rage, instead of behaving like a rational being. It was easy, for instance, to warm his body, even amid the snow. Condrille had taught him that, when he was only a child. He concentrated upon warmth, sending it along his veins, down his muscles, through his very bones as he relaxed and breathed deeply. His eyes closed. In a short while they opened again, and he was no longer trembling with chill.

He strode confidently through the snow, up the edge of the island where bushes grew in profusion. There he habitually set snares for the hares that lived along the river, though they were fewer in winter than in warm weather. Though their tiny track was now deep in snow, one of his snares held a fat hare, its pink eyes glazed in death. Although it had obviously been dead for some time, the cold had not yet frozen its blood. It would be usable for his purpose, but a child would be so much better!

Into the snow before his door, he tramped a pentagram and marked over the track with the blood of the hare. Then he laid the small body in the center, between his feet. With all his strength, he willed his familiar demon to come to him. "Eloim, Essaim, frugativi et appellavi!" He said, his breath steaming in the frigid air. Again he said the words, adding a few syllables of a powerful Key for compulsion. There was a long moment of stillness. Then the air was troubled at a spot outside the pentagram. The shadow of a strange shape formed there.

"Why do you call me by day? Outside the proper place?" The voice was a rumble so deep it shook snow down from the twigs of the bushes and the stems of bare saplings along the stream.

Lallius faced it confidently. "I am in need of aid, locked out of my own place and without means of entering the tower where you have come so many times. There I have delighted you with offerings far better than this poor one, and will again if you help me. I require and compel you to go within this door and to remove the lock that holds it fast."

He lifted the body of the hare and placed it upon the line edging the pentagram, nudging it across with one toe. The inchoate shape bent over the hare and there was a shimmer. Without warning, both were gone.

Lallius stood inside his protection, waiting. This was not one of the Great Ones, of course, but even lesser demons were tricky and dangerous to deal with. He had often wondered why they came to the summonings of men at all. Surely the feeble compulsions his kind used could not actually force such beings to act against their wills.

Then he forgot his questions, for there came a scuffling beyond the door. Something creaked. Something cracked sharply. Something metallic fell loudly upon the stone floor.

The shape appeared beyond the pattern. "Is all well, Man?" it asked.

"It is well. Go hence. I require and compel you to return to your own place."

He heard something like a saturnine chuckle. Then the air was clear, the shape dissolved into the sunlight. Drained, as usual, by the summoning, reeling with exhaustion, Lallius moved to scuff out the marks of his pentagram and to cover the blood with fresh snow. Only when that was done did he approach his doorway. One more obstacle stood in his way, but this was one he had formed himself and he could cope with it.

Holding up his right hand, he called into it the power that made it glow, even in the bright light of day. Sparks formed at his fingertips. He shook them loose, flinging them against the door. When he touched his burning hand to the wood, he could hear the wooden bar sliding free, even as the bar across the woman's door had slid free the night before. He could control wood. It was metal that defied his power.

At last he was able to stagger up the stair to his rooms, trailing his unlikely garment behind him. The fires had long since died to ash, and his stiff fingers were slow with flint and steel. He grumbled at the effort, but he did not rekindle his hand—he had no energy left for such matters. Now he needed food and a long, long sleep.

When the fire crackled, he set a kettle on the hook to boil above the flames. Into that he put meat he had brought from the larder the day before. No thin soup would renew his energies today, he knew. He chewed at a chunk of raw venison while waiting for the meat to cook. This would have sickened him, back in his own world, he knew, but here he had been forced to take on the uncivilized ways of this place.

He slept on the hearth while the meat boiled. Seldom had he known such exhaustion, for he was wearied as much by rage as by the cold and his efforts on the wall. The drain on his strength required by the conjuration had taken the last of his energy. When he woke at the spat of boiling broth onto hot coals, he ate ravenously. Then he took himself off to his bed, though even as he moved something nagged at him. Had he fastened the bar across the tower door?

Yes.

Had he taken care that the fire could not set anything ablaze?

Yes, he had.

What, then, troubled his mind? Was there something outside that might threaten him? Something in the forest? Would the woman attack him? She was well able, he had learned, but how could he know? She was an unknown quantity. Yet he was not satisfied that she was the source of his unease.

He went to the window and opened the other half of the shutter. Leaning out, he gazed into the forest, toward the shelter she had used before. Using the very last of his energies, he tried to sense her presence, but he could not. Chill emptiness breathed from the hut.

Deeper in the wood, something stirred. Where? He could not tell, yet something unfamiliar had set its thought upon him. Such matters are always apparent to sorcerers.

# CHAPTER FIFTEEN

## THE GOING-THROUGH

All the preparations were completed. The rituals, the chants, the purifications were done, and both Runs-Bucks and the shamans were weary from the ordeal. All, however, still felt the power of their talisman; it had shown Runs-Bucks where he must go to save Two-Moons from her attacker. Such power was far more than even the most hopeful had dared consider, besides being far more than any potency ever achieved before by the efforts of the holy men.

Ase-karenna, the mother of Runs-Bucks, had made him new buckskins for this strange journey. She had lived up to her name by composing a new chant as she worked with the skins, and this was a comfort to her son. His mother, had she been chosen, might have been one like Two-Moons, for her dreams, even burdened as she was by daily concerns, often foretold matters of importance to both family and clan. Her songs held power, and Runs-Bucks felt this new one might well impart a blessing to his garments. Odatsehe had spoken privately with him for a long while. This was the day chosen for his going forth through that ghostly doorway. It was sooner than the old men thought wise, yet later by far than Runs-Bucks would have chosen.

He knew that Two-Moons had already fled from the

124

tower. This meant she was abroad in an unfamiliar forest, with animals she did not know and dangers she could not guess. Perhaps men, too, who were more dangerous than any beasts. Though he valued the advice of the old men, he felt that no plan suitable for this world might work in that one.

When Odatsehe was done, the two of them went out into the walled compound to meet Wathadodarho. He was surrounded by shamans, the Dreamers, and the Matrons. Most of the adults from all the clans were there, for this was an exciting matter. Arising as it had in the middle of winter's long boredom, it had aroused the interest of all, even those who were unconcerned with either Two-Moons or Runs-Bucks.

Now Runs-Bucks-Down was weary of advice and ritual. The talisman was in his pouch, secured to his waist by several sets of thongs. His pack was filled with pemmican and parched corn, a blanket made of light furs, his bearskin cloak, extra moccasins, an extra knife, and other necessities for traveling in unknown territory. All was ready, yet he must stand through another long round of talk and pipe smoking. To all appearances, he bore it patiently.

Wathadodarho must have seen the impatience in his eyes, however, for he drew matters to a close more quickly than usual. "And now we send forth this warrior, our brother, to make a journey unlike any ever made by an Onondaga. Our Dreams will accompany him, and our hearts' blessings. Farewell, Brother. Walk truly, aim well, and return to us soon."

Suddenly Runs-Bucks found himself free to go. The crowd melted away before his steps, most grunting some good wish as he passed. Once he was outside the paling wall, on the path, his heart thumped with excitement. His left hand gripped the talisman beneath his robe, even as his right held tightly to his flint knife.

By now it was late afternoon. For part of the day the

sun had shone through a high layer of clouds, but those thickened as evening approached. The trees swam in pearly light, and the snow looked as insubstantial as mist as Runs-Bucks hurried toward the tree against which Two-Moons had leaned. Once there, he turned his face to the direction from which he had come.

There he had gone through the door. There he must go again.

He lifted the pouch by the thong and held it against his heart. "Taonhiawagi, Master of Life, you have led my spirit past this doorway before. Now I hold in my hands the talisman, made up of the gifts you sent to each of our Dreamers. Lead me again through this terrible door, in my flesh, into the place which holds my brother Two-Moons."

He did not beg. As one still wearing human flesh, he had done all he could. Now the One who formed the world of the Onondaga must, if he would, take upon himself the task only he could accomplish.

Runs-Bucks felt no doubt as he walked forward, the new snow squeaking beneath his double moccasins. There was no shimmer, such as he had seen in his vision. At one moment he was striding between elms and maples forming the wood he knew. At the next, he stood beneath an oak larger than any he had ever seen. About him stretched a small clearing, across which a game trail threaded its way beneath the snow, winding between bushes and saplings.

He cast the net of his orenda abroad, meshing it with that of trees and shrubs and dormant grasses. Those fairly shouted her recent presence, much more recent than could be attributed to her first passing there days before. They also held a memory of another, tainted with alien power, who could only be the pale-faced man who had stood naked in the tower.

Runs-Bucks put the pouch back into its safe place, securing it well. Only through it could he and Two-Moons hope to travel back to their home from this place, he was certain. He sheathed his knife in its deer-hide sling. Stringing his bow, he set an arrow lightly in place and moved ahead, cautious as if he were on a raid against a dangerous enemy.

Once he found the river, he moved away from the path that ran beside it. Now he slipped through the edge of the wood, hidden from any who might watch from the tower or the forest beyond the stream. Nothing stirred on the path or on the frost-white expanse of the stream. He could hear faint chitterings and chirpings deep in the wood where birds must be feeding on weed-seeds, but no other sound reached his ear.

At last he saw the tall black structure he had seen in his vision. Knowing that Two-Moons was no longer there, he drew yet deeper into the forest, skirting the island around the tower at some distance. He settled into a sheltered spot among thick bushes to await nightfall. There had been no sign of her passing on this side of the stream, so she must have gone away to the other side into that other forest.

Here the day was little past noon, not mid-afternoon as it had been in his own country. The sun was hidden behind snow clouds, its disk a bright patch beyond the silvery layers. He estimated that he must wait here for a long while before darkness would fall. Yet he did not want to cross that white expanse and be seen by anyone in that tower.

As he waited, he wondered about these two worlds that touched at that invisible door. Time, he felt instinctively, was a bit different here. It was probably not the only thing that was strange and alien.

He allowed himself to doze, though cautiously and with one ear alert. Deer moved in the wood at his back, and he heard them paw aside the snow to reach hidden mosses and frozen grass. Small animals dropped nuts from the tops of the big trees deeper in the forest. Rabbits began to venture out into the snow, though only the bold ones left their burrows in such bitter weather. Those normal sounds registered upon Runs-Bucks' mind without arousing in him any sense of danger.

It was dark at last, or as dark as the snow light allowed the night to become. Flakes began to drift down from the low clouds, which helped to obscure the countryside, and Runs-Bucks hurried now, afraid a heavy snowfall would hide any tracks Two-Moons might have left. Crossing the stream well above the tower, he made his way swiftly down its other side until he came level with the black building. A dam of deadfall blocked the waterway there, and to his relief he saw a trail leading to it from a door in the tower. It was plain that the tenant used this as a source of fuel, for the track was worn plainly into the snow.

He stepped up onto the tangled mass of branches and logs and bent to lay his hand against the topmost tree trunk. She had been here—there a twig had shifted away from its original position, leaving a mark in the snow. Here the snow had been packed by the passing of a light foot. He traced the outline of the heel with his fingers.

So, she had gone this way. He backed away and gazed at the strip of snow at the end of the dam. One print, half obscured, marked its edge. Hers, for he knew her moccasin print as well as he did his own.

Now he again opened his orenda to the spirits of the forest. Those led him through the tree-lanes, north and east, until he stood beneath a tremendous tree. She had rested here—it tingled with her presence. Runs-Bucks looked up into the darkness and whispered, "Two-Moons-in-the-Sky!"

There was no reply. He called louder, but there was no answer. He moved around the sheltered area at the foot of the tree, finding the buttress roots, the still-warm stone of the fire-pit that told of her presence. He climbed into the branches, up and up, moving on until he found the spot where she had rested. She was no longer here, but the tree held a sense of the presence of others, strangers, and those overlapped the impressions he was seeking. Other people had come. She had waited until they left, perhaps.

He felt about. Here she had tied her pack and her robe, and they were no longer in place. Those others had not taken her away, for only she would have returned for her possessions. He understood her caution. Where men had come, others might also come. So she had gone away into this strange wood, seeking another shelter in which to wait.

It was now sooty-dark, the snow falling very fast. This was a better spot than most in which to camp. If he remained aloft, it was unlikely that anyone would find him, if such should return here. He would rest, now that he was in the same world with Two-Moons. His task did not seem now as hard as it had before. He took his blanket from his pack and wrapped it about him. Then he leaned into a comfortable crotch and settled for the night.

This time he slept deeply, after eating a bit of pemmican and thawing snow in his mouth for drink. Tomorrow, he thought, might be a very long day.

# CHAPTER SIXTEEN

## WHO STALKS THE STALKERS?

Two-Moons returned to the sheltered campsite after the two men were gone and she had checked to make sure they did not turn back. She cooked her hares and ate, but she had no intention of remaining there for the night. This sheltering oak was too well known to the local people, it seemed, to risk using. After eating, she secured the rest of her meat in a bag made of the animals' skins. She retrieved her pack and her outer robe, which was more than welcome in the cold of the night, and set out to track those two whom she had observed here. There would be neither rest nor security, she knew, until she was convinced they were out of this forest.

Casting her orenda abroad, she picked up faint traces. Even their breath had touched the trees, and their feet had tramped the grass beneath the snow. The night was growing colder, and now and again she heard the crack of some overburdened branch breaking in the deeps of the wood or some great tree freezing to the heart and snapping along the grain. Without the warmth of her thick robe, she would have gone into the last cold sleep, and dawn would not have awakened her.

She did not try to follow in the tracks of the two men. They had impressed her as being good foresters, and they might well have sensed pursuit. If they watched their back-trail, as any sensible warrior always did, they might well ambush her in this unfamiliar forest. Instead she followed the impact of their passing as she read the trees and the bushes along their route, keeping her own path at a distance from theirs. It was too dark among the huge trees to see anything but the glimmer of snow underfoot and a tangle of black trunks and branches.

As she followed, she began to sense something else—a miasma of death and fear. Yet amid it she sensed living presences as well. Using that sensing as a guide, she found herself approaching a cluster of buildings in a small clearing, and she knew her quarry had taken refuge there from the cold and the night. She felt their presence in one of the huts, set apart at some distance from the main huddle of the village, even before her keen nose caught the tang of smoke from their small fire. Between that hut and the forest lay unbroken snow, except for the tracks of their feet. Anyone approaching across the white expanses around the hut could be seen by a watcher, and those two would set a watch, she knew by instinct.

She stopped within the shelter of the last rank of trees and set her senses searching through the other houses there. She could hear nothing, even though those two must be together in their chosen hut. Only the smoke came to her nostrils, with a faint hint of rotted wood.

By the snow light she could see that many of the houses were roofless and more had lost portions of walls. The hut the men had chosen was the only unbroken shelter there. There wasn't the slightest whisper of wind. There were no animals, for any dog would have growled or barked at her approach. She stepped forward silently, scuffing her moccasin toes into the snow so it would not creak beneath her weight. Her bow ready, arrow nocked, she slipped around the forest edge, past the lone hut, and darted at last into the shadows lying between the ruined houses.

Here was shelter—a partial roof and a wall against the wind was more than she had found for shelter many times before. She had eaten, and she had her robe. If those men had indeed watched the back trail, they had seen no one, and they would surely not expect any tracker to be in this abandoned place. They were unlikely to search their own hiding place.

She found the tumbledown houses set in a square, all facing a wide open space, in the middle of which a large structure stood. It was almost as long as the longhouse and much wider. Like the tower, it was stacked layer upon layer. Though the roof was ragged and she could see the dim sky through gaps, the other layers should insure that the lowest would be protected from snow.

Two-Moons found an opening half blocked by a rotted door and picked her way toward it across stone blocks that the wind had scoured clean of snow. She trailed her heavy robe behind her to erase her track when she must cross a patch of white, as she had been doing since she left the tree line. Inside it was cold, of course, and dark, but she knew she could sleep here in some safety. She found a comfortable corner that was hidden from doors or windows. She pushed aside the debris of leaves and twigs that had collected there. Small lives were around her, the orenda told her, but only those of wood rats, chipmunks, and an owl, whose intent regard she felt when she crossed the wide chamber to reach her nook.

She arranged her big robe and set her bow and arrows conveniently at hand. Her knife she placed within her inner robe, and then she folded herself into the fur in a way that would allow her instant freedom, at need. As she drifted into sleep, she felt something niggling at the edge of her awareness. Something familiar...but it was too late. Her exhaustion had carried her into the dark deeps of sleep, and she could not rouse again.

The scutter of a mouse among the leaves on the stone

floor woke her. The room was filled with chilly gray light, once she uncovered her head and looked about. Without rising, she fumbled some of the cold hare from her bag and nibbled at it. This cold sapped the strength. Though small game did not hold enough fat to sustain her for long, it would do until she could find larger.

She had put her damp moccasins on the floor beside her. Overnight the dampness froze, and when she sat, she took them into her hands and worked the ice crystals free of the buckskin, leaving the footwear dry, though very cold. Two-Moons wrapped her inner and outer robes about her, then rose and listened to the morning. In the distance she could hear a dog barking, but it was so far away she knew there must be another village within earshot of this one.

There was again the tang of smoke in the air, and it occurred to her that if she could find the stair she might watch those in the hut from a place in which no one could possibly see her. She ventured across the floor again, avoiding piles of rubble from fallen walls. A stout stairway rose at the other end of the room. She went to its foot and stared upward. Though the steps were rotted, filled with gaps as far as she could see, the heavy timbers that held them in place seemed to be sound. She felt she might go up safely, if she put her feet at the junction of stair and wall—but not yet. First she must conceal all trace of her presence.

She hid her pack and weapons beneath the stair in a cubby filled with spider webs and dust. Then she pushed the debris back into her sleeping spot, which was entirely too clean to match the rest of the place.

The upward journey was not as hazardous as she had expected, but she found the upper story partially open to the sky, though most of the outer wall was fairly solid. She picked her way to the side on which lay the hut and peered cautiously through a crack.

Smoke rose from the broken chimney of the small building, and tracks told her that someone had been outside already, though the sun had not yet risen. She sank onto her heels, considering her options.

There was a vital matter needing a decision. She must watch the tower on the island, for whatever it was that Burning-hand intended, it would be there where he would work his magics. If these men also intended to observe the doings of Lallius, they might restrict her freedom of movement. She had to know their direction and their purposes before she chose her own course.

For the moment she must watch them and learn. Her present position was somewhat exposed to the elements, but there was little likelihood that it might be investigated by the two she watched. She could only hope they would proceed with whatever they planned, rather than sheltering in the hut to wait for better weather. A stir of movement caught her eye, and she peered again through the crack. The taller of the men, the one called Athol, came out and looked up at the sky as if judging the weather to come. He shook his head in disgust, seeing the low-rolled snow clouds on the horizon, and called something back to his companion. Then he moved toward the forest along the track the two had made the day before, checking on their back trail, as she had been certain one of them would do. The other came out of the hut before he returned, pulling the door tightly shut behind him. Smoke no longer rose from the chimney, and the man carefully smoothed out all the tracks around the shelter with a branch full of dried leaves. It was plain that those two were hiding too, and she wondered from whom they hid and why.

When Athol returned, they did not meet in the snow but at the edge of the wood. They turned their faces westward, toward the river and went forward together.

She watched them, moving around the upper floor of the house to keep them in sight until they disappeared in thick trees. Then Two-Moons descended as cautiously as she had gone up, retrieved her possessions, and circled back into the wood to locate their present route. They still headed west. When they crossed the little river, she moved back down toward the tower, keeping to the eastern bank.

She must keep a watchful eye on Burning-hand's stronghold while she waited to learn what must come.

A fallen tree offered shelter, not too distant from the island, and she built a scanty fire in the root-hole and heated the rest of the last hare. Afterward, she covered the ashes deep with snow, smoothing it so as to seem undisturbed, and removed herself to a spot from which she could see the doorway of the tower, which was on the south side of the structure.

Night fell. Burning-hand's light shone through the cracks of the shutter to his work room. Two-Moons mused, wrapped in her heavy robe, upon the strange utensils the white-faced man possessed and the things he did. The books—she was still intrigued by the thought of marking down words and ideas for another to see and understand. It was a magical thing, one that she would have liked to learn and to take back to her people.

As she half-slept, half-watched through the night, something again niggled at the back of her mind. Though her thought was entirely focused upon the tower and its inhabitant, her orenda still hinted at a familiar presence, yet Two-Moons was too preoccupied to guess what that might be.

Already, she had tried to follow her own trail back into her home world, but that had been impossible. Surely it would be just as impossible for anyone to come here from that other. She must wait. All her instincts told her that some kind of help would come, but that must be left to the will of Aireskoi and Taonhiawagi.

What human being could possibly help her here?

# CHAPTER SEVENTEEN

## THE ENEMIES OF ULRIC

Thomas Falconer felt uneasy from his scalp to his heels. He had hunted these forests freely in the days of Osric, the father of Ulric, who now ruled here, knowing that the beloved lord did not begrudge a poor man food for the winter. He had poached these woods since the death of Osric, despite Ulric's ban on the taking of game by any except his own household. His peasants might starve, for he had no care for any except himself.

Thomas had believed he could count upon his fingers all those who might dispute his right to his old haunts. The alien arrow that had struck the tree between his head and Athol's had shaken him more than he would care to let Bladeford know. Not only was the shaft wood unusual, but the fletching was a strange design, feathered with unknown plumage. He'd pointed these out to his companion in order to hide from himself the terrible strangeness of the thing. The point was hand-chipped from some hard, glassy stone, primitive compared to their metal arrowheads, yet expertly shaped and deadly.

Thomas's grandmother had told tales of small people who lived beneath the hills and used such things, small in size to match their own stature. This was not small, however, but full sized, the shaft near a good cloth yard long. A full-grown adult had pulled the bow that sent it deep into that tree trunk.

He had wanted to dig the thing out and bring it along to study, but he knew that would bring unwanted questions from Athol. He had left it stuck in the tree, and he hoped that neither it nor any match for it would seek him out again. The night in the warm hut had eased him a bit, and when Bladeford insisted upon moving into the forest west of the stream and north of the tower, Thomas did not argue. He had felt all through the night that eyes searched for him, even through the walls. He had dreamed of a misty warrior who skulked at his heels, of an endless wood and of arrows that whizzed out of nowhere to thunk into living wood with a voice of terrible warning.

Of course, he might have gone back to his village and his middle-aged wife and their brood of half-grown young ones. No one hunted for him, for he had poached so shrewdly that not even Ulric's stewards suspected it was his hand that took so much forbidden game beneath their noses. Yet he could not return to his own place and leave his companion alone. He owed a great debt to Athol.

Bladeford was the son of Osric's brother, and Thomas was only the brat of one of the lord's falconers. The two had not been too near in age, for Athol was some years the younger, yet they had been drawn to each other from their early years. Both were eager hunters; deer and boar and wolves had fallen before their arrows and spears. Their friendship had gone deeper than their fathers would have approved, had they known of it.

Then Athol was sent to France and Thomas married and began begetting his large family. It was inevitable that when Ulric succeeded his father and times grew lean, the hunter would return to hunting, be it forbidden or not.

He had been caught only once red-handed at his poaching. It was Athol, newly returned to his old home, who caught him, and turned his eyes away from the slain deer and the bloody-handed man busy gutting it. When a forester came after the young nobleman, Athol claimed the deer as his own kill and commended Thomas for field-dressing it for him.

"I want only the hide and the head," he had said. "Give the meat to Thomas for his family."

It was no small thing he had done for his old friend. Thomas would have been racked and hanged, leaving his family to starve and freeze, for they would have been cast out of the lord's village into the forest to die. Thomas felt himself bound to Athol by ties no strange unease could break. Now he followed Bladeford through the forest, knowing that matters were presently much different from the situation when Athol returned from France. Athol himself was banned from their ancestral lands by his cousin, for he had protested against Ulric's new rules and harsh requirements for the common folk. In turn, Ulric had hinted that Athol must be base-born himself or he would not take an interest in such low people. Their quarrel had grown bitter, with such fierce heat that the two had parted with rash vows of vengeance.

Only the fact that Ulric had gone courting allowed the two of them to move about his fiefdom with some freedom. The stewards and foresters had no quarrel with Athol; indeed, they were grateful to him for many past favors. They pretended not to see him if they encountered him by chance. Thomas could not understand why Athol was so set upon prying about his cousin's lands. With Ulric away, what could they do against him? And if he came home, it would be worse.

"We must come within eyeshot of that tower from the west," Athol said, breaking into Thomas's thoughts. "Do you know a spot where we can see, yet where we will not be seen?"

Thomas mused for a moment. Then he said, "There is a thicket where I used to set snares. It should serve," and he led Athol there, arriving before mid-day.

As they came in sight of that black tower, Thomas's heart was filled with grief and anger. Two of his children had gone into the wood and had intended berrying along the stream; they had gone too near the tower. Those who watched the paths to and from the village had not known they would cut back toward the river and so did not stop them. Only Thomas's tracking skills had told him the sad tale. Their small footprints ended at the sandy verge of the stream, just opposite the western side of the island. He had crossed the stream, dog-paddling desperately, and hammered on the oaken door of the tower. No answer had come to his knocking. He watched for days, but aside from a strange colored light shining from a high window he had seen nothing. The children were gone. No trace of them was ever found again.

Now he realized that Athol's plot against Ulric must concern the wizard and his tower, in some way Thomas could not guess. Anything that troubled that black-hearted villain was to his liking, let the risk be what it might. At this point he needed to know what Athol's purpose might be, in order to help him effectively.

Once they settled themselves beneath a snow-banked hawthorn, their feet well wrapped against the cold, there was nothing to do but watch and wait. Thomas felt this was a good time to ask. "'Tis time, Athol, to tell me your plan. I canna help if I know nothing. How can worrying this wizard hurt yon Ulric? I've no objection to destroying either or both, but I canna see the connection."

The tall man's gray eyes half closed. The lines about his mouth became a grimace. "I've been working it out as we moved, Thomas. Now I think I have the plan in hand. Look you—that island is freehold, you say. Once it was the property of a powerful man of doubtful habits, and now it is the home of another such.

"This one holds it by tenancy, in fact if not in law. Possibly in both, yet I have a doubt of that. He has been left to his own devices for generations, which is in itself not a natural or a human thing, and he is spoilt to getting his own way here because all fear to meddle with him. He looks for no interference from noble or commoner." Athol cocked his head to look through the bushes at the tower.

"If he is all you tell me, he knows well who owns the neighboring lands about him. He must understand the common rules of courtesy between landholders, for he has lived by them for too long to be ignorant of them. What if he now is troubled, his peace broken, and his habits disturbed by unseen enemies? What will he think except that his neighbor has decided to take away his property? It is my thought that he has no legitimate right to that tower, for if he had, it would have been simple to present any proofs to my ancestors. That he has not done."

"But how will he connect Ulric with such troubling?" Thomas asked. "We are none of Ulric's, and we dinna look the part."

"But we can!" the other chuckled. "I have pilfered foresters' cloaks from his store, broidered with Ulric's device. I have stolen arrows from Ulric's men-at-arms, idling now while he dances attendance upon the fair Margaret. We may become a veritable army belonging to Ulric, harassing the wizard until he loses patience and wields his sorcerous weapons against my cousin. What think you?"

Thomas was a man of wit and wile and patience in dealing with game. Now he saw that such matters could be used in other ways, though he had never had much head for far-ranging planning. This intricate plot filled him with admiration. "No head such as yours did I ever know before," he marveled. "This may well work, Athol. We will come at yon tower from east or from west, from upstream or from down, at our choice. What say you to a fire-arrow in his windowsill as darkness falls? Might that not gain his attention, think you?"

The tall man laughed softly. "It might, indeed. If it

takes us a week or a month or a year, my friend, we will harry this wizard nest until swarms of stinging things pour out upon Ulric's keep and his men and, I devoutly hope, upon my cousin himself."

# CHAPTER EIGHTEEN

## The Air Is Filled with Enemies Unseen

Lallius had never been so furious in all his long life. The indignity the woman's escape had caused him still rankled within him. He was a sorcerer, a necromancer of great skill and power. His manipulations had never gone so far awry before, and he refused to accept this failure. Not only was the woman useless for trapping her own people into slavery, she was now gone from his clutches entirely.

He had spent a restless night and a more restless day after her escape. Though he still had a feeling that something approached, bearing ill intent toward him, none of his conjurings had offered any clue as to what that might be. Worse yet, he was not certain what he should do now. There was no chance of finding the woman in the forest, and he was not unwise enough to try. It was plain that the spirits at his command were in some manner inhibited from approaching her.

He wished, not for the first time, that he had a trusty human henchman to help him work his will in the physical world. That turned his thoughts once again to his original purpose. He needed slaves. The door he had created was in place, there on the other world just across the barrier of time. Why could he not pull through that door more of those dark-skinned people? Surely that woman was not the

142

only one with power. With cowed primitives to bend to his will, he could use them to find the woman, as well as whoever else skulked in the forest. Still, there was the possibility, remote but perhaps real, that others of her kind might be as intractable as she.

When night fell he was busy in his work room. He renewed the pattern drawn on the floor, lit the candles, and drank the potion prepared to stimulate his powers to the utmost. Once more he stripped and stood in the circle, focusing his will upon the spot in that other world where the ephemeral doorway still waited.

It was not easy. The world into which he reached was removed from this, a different segment of this planet, he had decided, beyond some strange window in time. Reaching across that gap was a draining task for the one who forged the link. He felt stretched to his limits, but he held fast to his flesh within the pattern, forcing his attention into that alien world.

Although in his own place it was almost night, in the other world it was still afternoon. He could see snow-clad trees whose tops were touched with weak winter sunlight. There was the path he knew to be the one the woman had traveled when she stepped into his trap. Now he realized that it had been careless to leave the trap unwatched. It might have brought him unwanted company, for he realized too late that his spell had been too broad in scope. It would bring to him anyone who moved along that trail who possessed even latent power. Already it had caught him one who was only trouble to him.

Now he seemed to hang, an invisible presence, behind that opening between dimensions. A woman came down the path, her back bent beneath a great bundle of wood. Two children, quiet and watchful, followed her in single file. To his astonishment he saw that the boy held a small bow and handled it as if skilled in its use. Once they were gone, the path lay empty for some time. Then a tall thin figure appeared among the darkening boles of the trees. There was a feel of old age about that shape, although it held itself erect and moved with ease through the snow to reach the path.

Now Lallius could see a long countenance, traced with uncountable lines. Bright black eyes flicked back and forth from treetop to path to the depths of the wood, never still, always alert. It was plain that this was not caused by fear but by old habit. The old man was a forest-runner of long standing, it seemed clear, automatically keeping watch on his surroundings. Lallius had seen other such men do the same in other dimensions than this, but still he studied him closely as he approached.

The man was very old, that was beyond doubt. Too old to possess the strength to defy a captor such as Lallius? That seemed likely. And he had wisdom, for it was apparent in his bright gaze, as well as his bearing. If he also had power, the transfer would be easy, and surely he would be skilled at things that would be useful to a wizard.

Yes, this one!

The sorcerer bent his will, opening the gateway wide. Even as he concentrated, there was a whish of sound and a glare of light back in the tower where his body waited. His focus snapped, and he found himself standing once more inside the pattern, his eyes blinking, his muscles quivering. What had brought him back without warning?

The fire had died to coals, and he bent above them to add fuel. The he realized that there was more light in the room than his candles and the fire could explain. Red flickered through the cracks in his shutters, and he went to the window. The stink of burning reached his nostrils as he pushed back the shutters and saw a flaming arrow sunk into the wood of the sill beneath the opening.

Gingerly, he reached for the shaft and pulled loose the arrowhead from the wood. It was wound with burning tow, which he pushed off the end with a knife from his work table. Curse that woman! How had she known that he was about to snare one of her people?

Then he looked closely at the arrow in his hand. He had examined those of his captive closely, marveling at their deadly efficiency, even though they were primitive things, stone-tipped. This was the kind of arrow he had known in his own world, as well as this one. Metal-tipped, fletched with goose feather, it had a longer shaft than that other. Not the woman's, that was clear.

But whose?

He pulled the shutters together and fastened the catch securely. Only a narrow crack remained through which he could see the river and the forest below. It was dark now, and there was no track marking the snow. Nothing could be seen in the edge of the trees, but did someone lie there, waiting to attack him? It must be this that he had felt so strongly, though he had thought it only worry over the escaped woman.

Lallius sank onto his chair, shaken and exhausted. The effort of opening the doorway wider had been a strain, but his unexpected return was a terrible shock. He knew he must sleep now, if he was to deal with this situation, whatever it might be, tomorrow.

He took his black cloak from its hook. Then, lying on the stained couch beside the door, he lay back and wrapped himself in it. Tomorrow he would use a seeking spell that he had learned from one of Condrille's old manuscripts, which had been forbidden to him when he was young. The magics he had used here so far were useful, but now he needed something stronger.

Drifting on the edge of slumber, he thought about his methods for the next day. A seeking spell must spring from his burning hand. The sparks would go out into the trees to hover above any spot where a human enemy might lurk. Then what? He was almost asleep now, but his mind worked on doggedly. The driving incantation? That was a dreadful thing, taxing the sender almost as much as the one against whom it was sent. Yet it was infallible, for an early king of his own city had driven the armies of a rival out of the walls, using such a spell. The sorcerer who devised that magic had been the first of a long line of royal wizards, rewarded often for their contributions to the ruler of his own lost country.

The routed army had run out of the valley and over the hills beyond it. They had run mindlessly down into a plain that led into desert, waterless and terrible, and their bones still slept there, he did not doubt. If there had been a sea at hand, he felt that the old king might have chosen for them to drown, but a desert was just as effective.

Where would he drive those who hid in his forest? Toward the village—that luscious village that had removed itself beyond his reach? No, there they might escape. These were human, and as such they were fit meat for his demons.

He would drive them toward his own tower, where they would find themselves welcomed guests. Not since those two children had he gleaned suitable prey from the land about him, and he hungered for their pain as his demons hungered for the effluvium rising from their souls.

First, however, he must make certain that they could not escape, as his late captive had done. Tomorrow, with the dawn, he would secure all the shutters so well that mere human hands could not open them. He would check all the bolts on all the doors, and he would replace any decayed bars with solid ones.

If a lone woman could bring such inconvenience into his life, what might occur with men?

He sighed deeply, his mind quieting. Yet his dreams were filled with fleeting glimpses of a tawny-skinned woman holding a bow. Something inside him shivered to think that she walked at large, beyond his control.

# CHAPTER NINETEEN

## OKTON-IYO COMES

Okton-iyo had been very restless since Runs-Bucks departed through that eerie doorway. He could not remain sitting in the longhouse with the other old people, gazing into the fire and telling occasional stories or jokes or accounts of old battles and hunts, while those of his blood walked in peril. When the sun came out in the afternoon, he went into the forest with his bow, though he expected to find no game so near the village. The women and children had spent the clear day in gathering wood for the fires, and where children expended their energies, game fled.

He wore his favorite cloak, a thick bearskin, nearly white, which was very rare and precious. When he was disturbed, it somehow comforted him.

He wandered about, checking game trails, testing the thickness of ice on the brooks, looking now and then toward the Mountain as he came to a clearing that gave a glimpse of it. Yet as the day waned, his uneasiness grew. Something would be required of him, though he could not think what it might be.

It was Runs-Bucks who had been entrusted with finding Two-Moons. Only he held the talisman that assured his return to the home of his people. What might be needed from an old man whose days of hunting and war were far behind him?

As he turned back toward the trail that led to the long-house, he saw Aronhia and her two children returning along it toward the village. He slowed his pace, for he was in no mood for talk, and Aronhia was one who talked too much and to little purpose. When she had disappeared around a bend in the trail, he stepped onto the path and turned also toward the village.

Then he saw the doorway of his vision. For an instant, it shone forth against the darkening forest, as if its edges flickered with cold flame. Okton-iyo was not a fearful man. In his long years of life, he had seen much of living and dying, of pleasure and pain and war. Now that he neared his own death, he found that nothing shook him from his interior calm. Not even the terrible white face that hovered like a mist behind the doorway could make him slow his step or change his expression. If this was the thing he must do, he would do it without hesitation.

Suddenly the face was gone, whisked away as if by magic, leaving a faint outline of the door traced upon the air. The old man hurried forward, his bow ready, an arrow on the string, and stumbled through the opening into snow that was deeper and dryer than that in his own forest. This was an alien wood, and he faced a tremendous oak tree.

A path lay before his feet, and he settled his cloak firmly about his shoulders before striding forward. Although night lay thickly about him, the snow light allowed him to see enough to avoid deadfall and stump-holes and other obstacles in his way. He came to a stream, after some time, along which another path led along the verge. Before he had gone far he saw with his own eyes the tower Runs-Bucks had envisioned. He automatically edged into the trees flanking the path as he approached the black shape rising against the snow-clad trees beyond the stream.

Slowing, he looked about. Then he moved deeper into the forest to find a tiny clearing. In it stood a shelter much like those he had built for himself, all his life, when caught out in a blizzard. A good omen, he knew at once, for it had the feel of his own kind about it. He moved to enter it, then turned about and found a spot from which he could see the tower. A slender crack of light shone high in its side. Someone was there, but the mesh of branches between that place and the hut was too thick to allow anyone to see if he approached the shelter across the little clearing. Was this the place where he must wait to be shown his purpose?

His heart felt at rest for the first time since he watched Runs-Bucks walk away into the trees. This was the place. He fumbled for his pouch of holy items and took it from its thong at his waist. Then he crawled into the rude hut and wrapped the bearskin about him, from face to feet, until he seemed only a mound of silvery fur, quiet in the darkness.

Once warmed a bit, he opened his pouch and touched each item within it. There was the tooth of the first bear he had killed as a youth. The pebble he had seen in a vision and waked to find staring up at him from a stream bed was there also, its white oval centered with rich brown, like an eye. All the experiences that had been important in his life were represented there by small things easy to carry. They formed his life and represented its power.

One by one, he caressed them. A chant rose in his throat, and he let it come softly into this strange world. "Aiee, Taonhiawagi, Master of Life, sender of all that is good into the forests and the mountains, hear my song...." The ancient hymn came automatically to his lips, and his thin old voice rose eerily, though he knew there was no one there to hear.

"Strengthen the hand of the warrior, the spirit of the Dreamer, the judgment of the Matriarch and the Sachem.

149

Send Aireskoi to guide the feet and the arrows of the hunters of game and the fishers in the streams.

"Shield us from the False-Face and all evil spirits of the wood. Taonhiawagi, Master of Life, hear my prayer."

In the tower, Lallius stirred uneasily in his sleep. The two men who had sent the arrow toward his window felt a strangeness in their bones. Two-Moons woke and sat, in her hiding place in the forest to the east, and Runs-Bucks felt a stirring in his heart. He almost guessed its cause.

But the old man had gone into the trance of a Dreamer, the chant coming without effort as he wandered the ways of the spirit. Not until his task was done would he wake, there in his cocoon of bearskin. Beneath the fur, clutched in his wrinkled hand, the stone eye stared into darkness, watchful and intent.

# CHAPTER TWENTY

## The Drawing-In

Runs-Bucks dreamed. When he woke, the dream was just below the surface of his thought, out of range of his memory, like a fish just too deep to catch with the hands from an eddy in a stream. Now and again he would catch a glimpse of it, but it would slip away too quickly to grasp.

This was a day when matters would move swiftly, he knew in his spirit. Before dawn brightened the east to pewter-colored cloud, he was well away from the tree where he had slept. Now he followed the track of Two-Moons, for she had not tried to conceal it as she moved through the forest. In turn, she had been keeping an eye upon those whom she had watched at the tree, for he could see where she had stood, sensing the trees and the brush for traces of their passing. He did the same when he infrequently lost her trail.

When he came to the edge of the ruined village, he stopped and sent his sensing outward again. She had been there. The shadow of her orenda still hung in the air, but she had gone away again. To watch those others out of sight? There were two deep tracks heading westward toward the stream he had crossed. At some distance to the south he found Two-Moons' trail, which shadowed those she followed for a long way before turning back toward the tower. She was going there.

Now he would no longer have to track her. He set his face toward the island where the tower stood and strode rapidly through the heavy forest. As was the way of his people, he made almost no sound as he moved, so he heard the newcomers to the wood long before they could have detected his presence.

They came from the northeast, trampling the snow-laden bushes and vines and talking in gruff voices. He could hear their words, although they meant nothing to him.

Now he must hide his track. Runs-Bucks cast backward for a short distance and swept the snow with a leaf-laden bough to a point at which his trail seemed headed directly toward the south. He trampled it a bit farther before stepping backward in his footprints.

Once that was done, he climbed high into a tree and looked toward the source of the noise, though the newcomers were still too far away to see, hidden among the thickly laced boles and branches.

Two-Moons, he knew now, would be near the tower. He could not know her reason, but he trusted her instinct. He wondered if these men also made it their goal. If so, she must be warned of their approach, or she might find herself in danger. He knew as well as she that strangers were more likely to be enemies than friends.

He slid out of the tree into a tangle of shrubbery. When he emerged from the tumbled snow amid the bushes, he again pulled his cloak after him, swishing it loosely to fill in his trail in the sift of new snow lying atop the older, hard-packed snowfall.

The going was slower, and he had not moved out of earshot when the two passed behind and to the north, moving westward, as those other strangers had done. Their tongue was strange, but he had learned long ago to read men by their look and their actions.

He circled widely, risking leaving a detectable trail, and settled into a thick clump of brush farther to the west. If they held their present course, he would be beside their line of march. He would look at these men. He might learn something, and at the least he would know them again. When they passed at last he found he was not very near their path after all. They spoke without caution, their words ringing loudly through the trees, as if only they had a right to be in this forest. It was plain that they expected no enemy, either before or behind them.

The alien syllables were clear in the cold air. It was frustrating not to understand the words, for he felt that the men spoke of matters that he should know about.

"They sheltered snug last night. Didn't go east from the village, so it's clear they headed westward. I read it thus, yet they cannot be fleeing from us. They cannot know we are here. They have some other game afoot, you can wager upon it. Athol was always a deep one, Lord Ulric. He has reason to meddle with your affairs.... He ventured to return as soon as he learned you had gone a'courting. He'll not be pleased to learn of your return."

"My cousin will be far less pleased when I catch him," rumbled a deep voice. "I'll gut him and hang him to season, Holt. As I did the poachers in the high forest, you recall?"

"That would go ill with the peasantry, Lord. He has feathered his nest with them, holding himself up as their defense against your rule. While you are by rights their Lord, still it might be best to leave a beehive unstirred. Even the lowest and most humble bee can sting hard when it feels itself threatened. I have advised you for many a year. Indeed, since your father's death I have given you my best. I'd say bind him and send him to the monastery at Twyvale to be held in solitary penance for the rest of his life. A dead man collects legends and followers far more readily than does a living one."

"First we must catch him, before we can dispose of him, however it is done," said the first man. "My instinct says that we should cross the stream and cast about the forest west of the tower that stands on the island. God rot that magician! He sits like a carbuncle on my rump, in the midst of my clean forest. May the Devil prod my great-great-grandsire, who let my island go as freehold. I'd give much to rid myself of both Athol and Lallius, Holt, and more to rid the lands of that wizard."

Runs-Bucks saw the other man stop and turn to stare at the speaker. He strained to hear the tone in which he spoke his next words. "Might it be…might it be, indeed, that yon Athol intends to stir the magician against us? To set him ablaze with enmity?

"Your emblem is not hard to imitate, My Lord. The arrows used by our men-at-arms are easy to come by, for they tend to be careless about hunting out those they lose in the wood. What if he hopes to stir that sorcerer to send his spells buzzing about our ears?" The tone held discomfort, almost fright, Runs-Bucks thought.

"I have known Athol, as I have you, since you both were children. I know the way his mind goes about solving problems. This would be a thing he could think about doing, and it would be something he would take delight in setting into motion."

Now they were moving out of sight, and their voices grew faint. Still Runs-Bucks strained to hear and interpret the strange sounds. Something disturbed the older man and was beginning to disturb the younger as well. Still, he did not dare to move from his shelter, for the older man moved like one who was completely at ease in the forest. He would note any unusual sound or motion, Runs-Bucks felt certain.

"Perhaps. We shall go and see, Holt. Go warily and secretly, eh? If Athol is settled into some snug burrow within earshot of that tower, I shall hale out my men and winkle him out, if I die of it. Mayhap, while I am about it, I shall also root out that wizard from his tower. I do not have the awe of him that my ancestors felt."

Then they were gone beyond earshot, though a faint mumble came to Runs-Bucks for a few moments more. Soon their voices died in the distance, and only then did he emerge from his hiding place and look after them. If only he had known their tongue! But it was as unlike Algonkian as it was unlike the Huron language forming the roots of all the Iroquoian tongues of the Kanonsionni. These men were a breed completely unlike any he had known in his own place.

If the words meant nothing to him, however, the tones and attitudes of the speaker told him much. One was a sachem of some kind, the other a lesser man. A shaman, perhaps, or an adviser...a Dreamer? He had the bearing of one who was used to being heard when he spoke, yet though his voice held the tones of counsel, it also had contained that edge of fear, as if he could not quite trust the man to whom he spoke.

Probably his advice, whatever it was, had been sound, for the man's orenda was true, unweakened by base matters. The other, however, was a different sort. In him Runs-Bucks sensed a careless cruelty that went far deeper than that of even the most callous young warrior. His orenda was not a stable matter, but filled with unsteadiness that must reflect rapid changes of purpose and conviction. The voice also made the heart shiver in his breast, for it was filled with such complacency, such conscious power, that it was fearful to hear.

No sachem among the Kanonsionni had such power over the members of that League. Those who came to the leaders for advice and judgment came of their own will. For only by the consent of the Onondaga did their chiefs rule, and only by the will of the people, as exercised by the Matriarchs, did the chiefs continue their rule. Otherwise they would be removed, as many had found in the past.

Now Runs-Bucks must move swiftly to find Two-Moons, for she could not know that these others approached. Unless she had sent her orenda afar across the forest she would be unaware that others were coming toward the tower. Here, neither of them knew the ways of those living in this world. It was best to remain unseen and unheard by those who belonged here.

He ranged cautiously but rapidly down the wood beside the stream, keeping the snow-covered ice in view, while remaining well within the trees. When he saw the tower thrust above the trees, he sent out a cautious sensing. There was the feel of Two-Moons close by. Hiding his track carefully, he closed upon the spot where she hid. When he came near, he called like an owl, very softly, with the flutter at the end of the call that told anyone of his people that danger was near.

For a moment there was complete silence; then the squeak of a field mouse rose from a clump of bushes completely covered with snow. The tangled branches quivered slightly, and a single glimpse of a brown face peeped forth. Two-Moons' black eyes shone from it, widening as she recognized Runs-Bucks-Down.

Still silently, the warrior picked his way to that clump of bushes and slid beneath the concealing branches, displacing only a little of the snow. Once he was concealed, they sat knee to knee, face to face, and Runs-Bucks held out his hand. Her strong fingers gripped his for an instant. Then she put her lips close to his ear and whispered, "So it was you who came! But how did you manage to come at all? The door was gone when I went back to seek for it to return to our own place."

Sitting there in the chill, warmed by her presence, he told her the story of his visions, of the talisman, and of his journey between the two worlds. It seemed strange, even as he spoke, but her expression told him she understood him, without question and without doubt. She had traveled this road before him and knew more about its perils, he was sure, than he.

When he completed his tale, with a description of the men he had watched in the wood, she took it up and gave her own account of the things that had happened since she left the village. When compared, the two stories formed a pattern, though neither of them could quite understand what it meant.

Runs-Bucks' instinct told him there were powers at work here that were beyond their understanding, so alien were the purposes they pursued. No answer to the puzzle could they find, for they had too little information about those who lived in this strange place. The one clear thing, they agreed, was that Burning-hand held in his dark heart some grim purpose for their people.

"I have felt that doorway come into being yet again," Two-Moons said at last. "When you came, I was far away in the forest and did not know, but as I slept in the wood, waiting to go on after those I followed here, suddenly that door admitted someone once again. I felt it in my spirit. Someone came through it, though whoever it was, his own orenda was overshadowed by the power of that spell. I could not name him, but he was one of our own people."

She stared into his eyes and said, "Even as I tried to feel who this might be, a fire arrow struck the tower, coming out of the forest west of the stream. I could see the glare of the blaze, though that window was hidden from me by the curve of the tower.

"Those I followed through the wood meant ill to Burning-hand, I know, for I learned enough of their strange tongue from the wizard to make out many of their words. It is good to have other enemies of the sorcerer at work, for I have come to believe that he wants others of our people here to do his work and perhaps to sacrifice to his dark gods. Why else would he have set that trap in our forest?

"He is one who cannot willingly work for himself, as I saw when we lived together in that tower. He is neither a witling nor a cripple, simply one who desires to live on the labors of others. And to do other things...wicked things that harm people."

Runs-Bucks grunted agreement. "I know. It was my call that woke you to your danger, there in the tower when he came naked into your sleeping place."

She nodded, a faint smile hovering about her lips. "Even as I acted, I felt a familiar presence, and knew that someone I knew had warned me. Only that warning gave me the time to escape from him, and for that and many other matters you have my thanks, Runs-Bucks."

He stared through the snowy branches at the day, which was now dwindling toward evening. The clouds had thickened considerably, although no new snow fell as yet. At the edge of the west, the sun lit the cloud cover to rose, but in the east, above the wood, the sky was already dark.

"It will soon be night," he said. "What should we do, Two-Moons? What does your Dream tell you?"

"In my dream, I saw strange things happening in that tower," she replied. "Men in bright, hard shells battered at the door. Arrows flew like flocks of birds; lances drew blood. Many terrible things have happened in this place, but most of those were in the long past. Taonhiawagi has led my thought, showing me what is past and what is yet to come, though the picture is dark, blurred like the reflections in a flowing stream.

"Yet this I know. Men will attack that tower, and they will desire the blood of Burning-hand. His blood is ours, Runs-Bucks. He has wronged us and would have wronged our people. Your talisman—will it take us back to our own place, do you think?"

"So say the wise ones of our people," he grunted. "My own vision, as well, tells me that this is true."

She nodded decisively. "Then we must be within that

tower before those who will come can break into it. We have a night, a day, and part of another night, if my dream is true, to find a way to enter it. Once inside, we must hide ourselves in one of the empty lower parts, where Burning-hand seldom goes. We must wait for the chance to take him captive and lead him away with us. By then others, lusting for his blood, may make him more willing to take our path than to remain and face them. Still, that place is secured well. The door is barred with wood, as well as that metal lock. I must think hard to find a way to enter it without his knowing we are there."

Runs-Bucks nodded, his heart cold in his breast. Unobtrusively, he felt of the talisman, secure in the pouch at his waist. There lay the key that could take them home again. If the Dreams were true, it might happen. If the visions had not lied, and if Taonhiawagi willed their return....

If and IF and IF.

He shivered as he sat, but he was a warrior of the Onondaga. He was not to be ruled by fear.

# CHAPTER TWENTY-ONE

## Lallius Casts a Spell

The sorcerer had gone about his tower, fastening shutters, closing the lower door with its wooden bar, and finding another lock to add to its security. He even brought the other three bars, unused for decades, out of the storeroom and slipped them into the rusty loops on door and frame. In addition, he went outside and stood upon a stool to nail the shutters fast, as high as he could reach.

Never did it occur to him that he might be wise to secure the inner doors closing off the rooms that let into the tower shaft onto the landings. He did shoot a few exterior bolts, almost at random, but it was with no sense of danger from those empty spaces. The upper shutters he closed, though he did not believe that anyone could climb the tower wall upward to pry them open. That would be far too mad an attempt even for the woman who had gone down that wall.

By nightfall he was satisfied that if his prey entered the tower, whoever that person might be would be at his mercy. He had left nothing to chance, for the woman's escape had shaken him.

Centuries past, when he had been the young Osperre in that valley lit by two moons, he had never tired of the rituals attendant upon sorcery. The cadences of the incantations had excited him, and the drawing of the protective ellipses, which here had become angled diagrams, had warmed him with enthusiasm. This excitement had remained with him for many years, and his association with Albertus had reinforced it. He too had been absorbed in his calling, and it was as much a part of that long-dead master as his bones and his blood had been.

Yet now Lallius was two centuries old, and not only had his body begun to protest at the cold and the strange efforts he required of it, his spirit also felt threadbare and unready for great efforts. It was, however, necessary, if he was to survive and continue his way of life. He must have slaves. For that purpose, he needed the aid of those ancient spirits to whom the scent of ebbing life and the flavor of a newly freed spirit were delightful. If he had those two strong men whom he had felt present, now sheltered in the wood—if he could subdue and control them—they could help him to pull through his doorway enough of the woman's people to serve him well and to feed his spirits for a long time to come. But first he must compel them into his tower.

As darkness drew in beneath a sullen sky, he stood at the west window and kindled his burning hand. He had opened his shutter partway, though he kept himself sheltered from any chance arrow. As the old chant rose in his mind, he called upon the power it summoned, needing no longer even to speak the words. The glow of his fingers, increasing moment by moment, set shadows to dancing about the room, warring with the candles he had lit. When the spell was most potent, he stepped to the window and pushed back the shutters. Shaking his fingers, he spun a flight of sparks into the air.

For an instant they hovered like a swarm of fireflies, making bright patterns against the darkness. Then they shot forth, tacking back and forth above the treetops and casting about after some trace of the lives they sought. Almost beyond his eyeshot, a group paused in mid-air and drifted downward to circle above a spot that he could not see even from the tower.

Those he hunted were there, he knew, below the candent halo of flames sent from his hand. Turning back into his laboratory, he collected his wits and settled his spirit. It had been a very long time since he used the driving spell, and even then it had been only an experiment. It was a dangerous undertaking, for it was not selective. One must take care to know who might be caught and compelled by it, and in his own world that had been of prime importance. Here, it was a matter of indifference.

He went again to the window and looked out, to find that the sparks were swarming through the night, coming back to be absorbed again into his flesh. He noted without interest that one small group was not returning, moving instead away to the north. But he was busy recalling the next spell in this sequence, knowing that such a small loss of energy would not trouble him at all.

Now he began to chant the old words, focusing his mind, moving his hands in the patterns of the ritual. His feet automatically paced, precisely within the figure he had drawn upon his floor, almost in a dance, as the spell progressed. A ripple of uneasy sound came through the glass from the forest. Birds called sharply and small beasts moaned and grumbled, troubled in treetop and lair. Everything living in the wood would be brought to his door, to be sorted out at his own leisure. The chirpings and growls drew nearer, as the creatures were compelled from their places and driven out into the cold night.

Among them walked a pair on two feet each. The men he had sought cursed and struggled as they neared the tower, unable to resist the compulsion of the spell. Lallius felt their desperation as they came, for his spell had them in its net. Though the chant did not alter, the dance changed, became more rapid, as the sorcerer smiled and sang. Two lives were his for the taking! Two strong men would resist the pain of his rituals for a long while, living after weaker people would have died, feeding the spirits that craved their suffering.

Warmth rose in the sorcerer for the first time in a long while. He would be able to accomplish a major Calling, one that would subdue the escaped woman and reinforce his control over all that he hoped to do.

As his victims approached, he backed through the room, one step at a time, never altering the pattern of his step, until he was outside the heptagram he had drawn. He danced across the landing and adapted his steps to the stair, keeping to the time and the pattern. Then he was down at the door, whose bars he drew and whose locks he unclasped. The spell was about to be completed.

He shot the bars into their sockets and pulled the heavy door wide. Standing outside, he stared toward the wood, from which hopped and scuttered and trundled and paced a stream of small, sleepy creatures. Hare followed chipmunk. A fox loped lazily, half-asleep, after a badger, which was moving grumpily along among a group of bewildered deer.

Behind those came the men, one tall and young, the other short and tough and older by some years. Lallius felt his grin grow upon his face, stretching muscles unused to smiling.

It had been so long since he sacrificed such strong victims! Their eyes were wide in faces grown pale between their smudges of grime. Their gazes strained toward Lallius, though they could not turn their heads as they passed him and entered the tower.

One of the deer clattered onto the flagstone floor and skidded before whirling to leap clear of that slick surface. Lallius waved the lesser creatures back with a commanding hand and closed the door against the tide of animals now washing against the tower.

A few hares and chipmunks littered his floor, and he

picked his way among them to follow his victims. They, forced by a will outside themselves, went up and entered the room next to his laboratory.

He laughed softly as he locked them in. He had removed the inner bars of that room, and they could not secure themselves against him, even if they found a way to resist his spell. They were his! And now his great work could begin in earnest.

# CHAPTER TWENTY-TWO

## AGAIN, THE TOWER

The two Onondaga sat together for a long time, calling upon their best judgment, as well as their orenda. Although neither had felt a whisper from Taonhiawagi or the guide of hunters, both Two-Moons and Runs-Bucks agreed that a time of Dreaming would give them strength and confidence.

By the time the day had darkened to cold silver twilight, Two-Moons was ready to try the outer door of the tower, although she knew it would be locked. And, of course, it was, but she motioned to Runs-Bucks to follow her as she edged around the wall.

She was searching the dark stone, in the dimness of the evening, searching for any reflection of snow light from the uneven courses of stone forming the structure. On the northeastern side, the wall had been eroded by winter storms for ages, their winds and ice chipping away the mortar between the stones. The slight unevenness there would be climbable, she thought.

Being the lighter, Two-Moons went up first, laying aside her weapons and her bearskin. Runs-Bucks caught her by the waist to lift her high toward the first good toehold. As he touched her, she felt a sudden surge of warmth and loss, but she put that from her mind and went to work, setting her moccasined toes into the cracks and seeking with chilled fingers for others.

A rotted edge of stone crumbled suddenly beneath her weight, and she gasped, gripping with her fingers like a spider on a wall. Cold sweat trickled down her back between her shoulders, and she held on, quite still for a moment. Then she quieted her breathing until her chest eased. Moving again cautiously, she found a solid spot and looked down to see Runs-Bucks climbing after her.

She thought of that ancient, insecure stone and his greater weight, but again she put away the thought. She might fall, or he might go down, but until such a thing happened they must go up, finger into crack, toe onto ledge, gaze fixed on the next handhold above.

It seemed hours that she climbed, going by touch alone once the sky darkened completely. But at last her sore fingers touched wood—a shutter. Those lower had been tried as they passed near them, but she had expected Burning-hand to fasten them, and she had not been disappointed to find herself correct.

Now she drew level with a window on the topmost floor, on the other side of the curve from that which had been hers. This would be one of the unused rooms into which she had never looked. She remembered the way in which the bar fitted into the slots inside. It was short work to lever it backward with the edge of her flint knife. The weathered wood split easily, even though she could spare only one hand for the work as her knife bit into the bar through the splintered crack.

She wiggled the blade, moving the bar inside a fraction at a time. Worrying at it patiently, she had the shutter loosed at last. She did not make the mistake of opening the leaf toward her, thus sweeping herself off the wall. She pushed the farther panel open and held onto it while she opened that nearest her. Then she called down to Runs-Bucks. "The shutter is wide. But take care, for this is old and rotten."

She could hear him breathing, as well as the faint scrabble of his movements against the wall below. She heaved herself over the sill, for this room had no glass casement as the sorcerer's window did. The room in which she found herself was cold and still, musty with dust and the smell of damp. Something moved, a tiny sound of claws on wood, in the corner, but she knew it was only a rat or a mouse which infested the tower. Turning, she leaned out to stare down into the darkness. She saw a dark bulk that was Runs-Bucks, and she reached to catch his hand and help him through the window. He was bulky with the burden of her weapons and his, as well as both their fur cloaks.

When he stood beside her she whispered, "Take care. The rooms I looked into are cluttered with many things, and it is hard to walk without making noise. Stand here by the window while I feel my way to the door. We will see if we can go into the tower from here."

Knowing the random way in which the decayed furniture was scattered through the abandoned rooms, she moved carefully, her skin-shod toes feeling for any obstruction, her hands outstretched, sweeping about to find anything taller. At last she reached a wall and a table. Another wall at the inner corner where this room met the next. The door.

"Come," she whispered in Onondaga, relishing the use of her own language.

Setting her ear against the musty door, she listened hard. She heard a distant mumble that sounded like Lallius at one of his endless rituals. A hand touched her shoulder. She reached up to take it in her own, and with her free hand she tried the latch of the door. But it was bolted, like the door that Burning-hand had secured behind her in the beginning.

"We might try another window," she said quietly.

"Perhaps he has forgotten to fasten the door to one of the rooms."

"No," said Runs-Bucks. "He is busy with something strange. Let us wait and see what he does, and then we may find a way to open this door, if you can give me a picture of the way that fastening works. I saw it in my vision, but it made no sense to me. While we wait, make me see the thing clearly, slowly, so that I understand its working."

She sank beside him to sit on the dusty floor, pulling her fur about her. She assumed her Dreaming posture, as did he, and they began this unusual task. "The hard stuff is metal, Burning-hand says. The stick of metal slips through two loops of the same material, which are set on the door and on the wall. So!" She took his hand in the darkness and formed with their two sets of fingers a fair approximation of the working of a bolt.

As she did this, the chanting on the other side of the tower landing grew louder. Bare feet pattered on wood, their rhythm matching that of the words. The sorcerer was going down the stair. Two-Moons saw him as plainly as if her eyes gazed at him, though it was her inner vision that followed him down the stair. For the first time since she had huddled under that bush and resisted the sparks, she felt a touch of compulsion.

She must move! Her knees twitched, and her feet, but she pulled her legs tightly into a crossed position and held onto Runs-Bucks' hand.

"He is calling someone, forcing them toward him. Do you feel that terrible need? It is not strong, but it is a desire to go where your will does not take you."

His voice was the merest breath in her ear. "Ai. A tugging, but easy to resist."

"I think it is stronger for those who belong here. Much orenda moves through this night. He is forcing someone. I wonder...." And then she felt something that had been in the depths of her spirit for some while. Familiar. A presence that was of her own kind.

"Do you feel it?" she asked. "One of our people is here, chanting the old hymn. His spirit is all about us!"

Runs-Bucks tightened his grasp on her hand. His voice was soft but joyful as he said, "Yes. It is Okton-iyo, my uncle. I know the texture of his orenda as I know my own or yours. He is here in this world, and this is something that Burning-hand cannot know, I think. This may set all his magics awry, for the sorceries of this world and of our own seem to be so different that they cannot work against each other directly. Yet you have been sheltered from this man by our own gods, according to your account."

She waited in the darkness beside her friend, her ears straining to hear what happened below. When the big door opened wide, it grated on the stone, the sound vibrating up the shaft. A time passed before they heard anything but dim and unidentifiable sounds. Then a muffled voice muttered and feet began to climb the stair. The big door was pushed shut again, with a shudder of wood on stone, and the sound of the bars being put into place was clear, echoing up the shaft of the tower.

They listened as the sounds of feet—two pair of heavy ones followed by bare soles—went to a room on the other side of the landing.

"He has caught those who hunted him," said Two-Moons. "He has shut them into the room next to that in which he tried to imprison me. Now he is, I think, in the room where he works, drawing patterns and lighting tiny torches and singing words that are not a part of the language he taught to me. He also looks into books, which are magical things into which people put marks that carry their wisdom or folly to eyes that have never seen the maker of those written words. He intends something terrible. I have seen those books, for he brought some into my own chamber.

"There are pictures there of hideous beasts eating children. Things worse than beasts drain the life from men and women who cry out in pain and terror. Even an Onondaga would scream, Runs-Bucks, if their bowels were being eaten by such horrible creatures. The Honorable Death is easy compared with those pictures."

"Then I must open this door," said the warrior.

She smiled. It was so like him, for calm good sense was his greatest quality. If he thought he might open that door, unfamiliar as it was to him, and loose the fastening on the other side of the wood, then quite probably he would do it. "Yes, it is time," she said.

She heard him fumbling in his pouch for the talisman he had shown her. Then he leaned his head near her own.

"Go into a vision with me. In that way I saw the warped face that came from this tower, and in that way I will move the lock, if Taonhiawagi and Aireskoi will aid me."

The Dreamer sat erect, focusing her mind. The Dream came slowly, but at last she felt her energies fuse with those of Runs-Bucks, as he reached toward his waiting vision. She closed her eyes against the dark and relaxed her body and her spirit, allowing all that she was to flow toward him and lend him her strength.

Behind her eyelids a picture formed; a bright hand, not the burning one of her captor but one lit as if from within, like sunlight behind ice. Strangely, it seemed to be on the other side of that door, near the bolt. Her breathing faltered for an instant, but she steadied it at once and followed that vision. More of her strength flowed out into Runs-Bucks. The hand touched the bolt and passed through it like mist.

A stronger pull on her energies made that hand burn even more brightly. When it settled to rest on the knob of the bolt, the knob moved. Not enough, as yet, but it moved. Beside her, Runs-Bucks gasped, his fingers tightening on hers until she almost cried out in pain. That other hand moved the bolt, slowly, slowly as ice forms or seed sprouts. The metal rod slid softly back along its track.

Metal clicked on metal, as it went into place against the baffle at the back of the device. The door sagged outward with a small sigh. It was now free, though still closed, and only a close examination would show it to be unlocked.

Runs-Bucks sagged against her, his weight on her shoulder warm and heavy. She was exhausted as well. First the climb, and then this draining effort had left her fit for nothing but sleep. She tried to shake off the lethargy, to rise, but it was too much. She pulled the fur close about herself and Runs-Bucks and slept.

\* \* \* \* \* \*

Across the landing Lallius slept as well, weary with his efforts. In the other room the two captives did not sleep at all, though they were now released from compulsion. They had found quickly that there was no escape from the chamber. Taking advantage of fuel made from rotting furniture, they used their flint and steel to kindle a fire in the hearth, and now they crouched before it, neither speaking. When their eyes met, they flicked away quickly. Neither wanted to see, mirrored in the gaze of the other, the obscure terror that was growing in both their hearts.

\* \* \* \* \* \*

In the forest, Okton-iyo sang on, his ancient bones unchilled, his old spirit undaunted. His voice was cracked now with use, but the chant still rose strongly from the hut beneath the great trees. Rising through the frozen night, it seemed to echo from the clouds that hung over the forest, the island, and the stream.

# CHAPTER TWENTY-THREE

## A Day for Summoning

Although he had intended to rise very early and begin his work on this most important of days, Lallius slept well past dawn. Once aroused, he found himself still groggy and disoriented for a time, for something had waked him, and he could not determine what it had been. He fumbled his clothing over his body, trying to find the thing that troubled his mind. Sitting on the side of his couch, he put his head into his hands. What was wrong?

And then the thing that had waked him brought him upright. A horn sounded to the north. It was a signal, without any doubt. Who summoned men-at-arms at such an hour and in this place that had been avoided for decades? So near his tower, this was unheard of, and the sound was very near.

He had remained untroubled for almost a century. Why should anyone change that status now? Might those whom he had locked into that next-door room be the cause of a search? They had, he remembered, seemed to hide. Those in the forest might be seeking them—or him? He thought of that as he paced about his room after rekindling his fire.

He prepared no food, for this day's work required fasting. Only his familiar spirits would be fed today, but to-night he would gorge on pain and terror, after his long

172

years of hunger.

The sun touched the tops of the trees west of the tower by the time he completed his last preparations. Two heavy racks, made of metal and fitted with leather cuffs and iron clamps for hands and feet, were in place. He had dragged them to opposite points outside the intricate new pattern needed for this proceeding. Candles waited for lighting in each of the twelve angles of interlocked hexagrams. When his diagrams were as perfect as painstaking effort could make them, he put his materials ready in their places. His incantations were a part of his very spirit now, needing no rehearsal, and he knew that once he had mixed and drunk the potion required for this transaction he would be filled with power.

He worked all morning and a part of the afternoon, mixing, measuring, straining, and refining the elements of that all-important mixture. It was not a simple spell, like that which opened his doorway into that other dimension. Only once before had he committed this act, on the occasion of the disaster with the royal infant. That effort had ended in catastrophe, because he was surrounded by people who did not understand what it was that he was trying to do. This time, he was determined that nothing would stop him from calling forth the most powerful aid possible from the dimension in which meddlesome spirits existed. No one could interfere, because not a single soul in this world would understand what he was doing.

Tomorrow, he would have slaves enough to serve him well and lives to sacrifice, when he rewarded those who aided him. Best of all, he would know that only he on this primitive one-moon world had achieved the Ultimate Arcanum.

Once he had poured the potion into a bottle and cleaned the alembic and his crucibles and vessels and put them away, he paused to rest. When he glanced out of his window at last (peering through a crack, for he had shut the wood against the chill of the day), he saw that the pale winter sun was dropping down the sky.

Already, the depths of the wood were purple with shadow. As he gazed into the trees, he thought he saw motion there, but no matter how he stared he did not catch another glimpse. Turning away, he lay on his couch, waiting for darkness to fall. This day his summoning would end in a night that would make history, even if only he could appreciate its importance.

Once he woke to hear quiet scratchings and pryings at the door where his captives worked cautiously to escape. He smiled. Not without magical aid could they leave that trap, for he had guarded it with spells. Only when they were taken out to be secured on the racks would they leave that room. And after that—they would have no strength for anything except their own sufferings. His pulse raced at the thought.

He dozed, dreaming that he heard soft steps on the landing, but he did not hear the bolt being eased back, for he was adrift in a cloud of smug achievement. The opening of that door beside his room, the whisper of feet on the landing was lost to him.

Lallius-Osperre was back in the valley of two moons, triumphant in the success of his most ambitious undertaking. No shadow of failure could possibly cloud the warmth of that dream.

# CHAPTER TWENTY-FOUR

## The Song of Taonhiawagi

By dawn Okton-iyo's voice had worn away and his chant was no longer audible, though he thought the words quietly as he sat, still wrapped in his silvery fur, waiting. The time for which he waited was drawing near, and his reason for being summoned to this place would soon come clear to his spirit.

Men moved in the forest by afternoon, he sensed, and they prepared to attack the tower on the island. That was clear to his orenda, alien though theirs might be. Their voices spoke meaningless words, but their selves burned plainly in his mind.

He waited still, as the day wore toward evening. In full darkness the attack would begin, for he read that in their actions. His own kind did not go to war by night, but he knew that there were those who did. These were obviously of that uncivilized kind.

None of the men in the forest noticed or paid attention to the rude shelter where he sat. Nobody stooped to peer into it, though the old man knew he would be invisible in the dim interior, his fur looking like snow to a casual glance. Just before sunset Okton-iyo uncovered his face, his bright eyes peering between cracks in the branch-twisted walls. The last of the sun struck the weathered walls of the tower, laying tracks of gold against the black stone. For a moment he saw a brightness gleam high in that wall, as if ice reflected the last light of day.

Then night descended. Feet crunched on snow about the hut, and shoulders brushed against branches. Weapons clicked, and he heard harsh breathing as the warriors readied themselves for the attack.

Was it the time for him to move? He closed his eyes and listened to the inside voice that had always guided him truly. No. Not yet.

The fate of that white-faced man was none of his concern, for he was here to protect his fellow Onondaga. He must wait for their signal, which would come, he knew, even though they could not know that he was present. He would be given a sign, for Taonhiawagi did nothing without reason.

Feathered fletches whispered as a fire-arrow darted across the sky, leaving a trail of sparks behind it. It struck the stone and fell harmlessly into the snow below, but another followed and another, until one thunked into one of the wooden shutters in a lower window.

It hung there, burning red against the dark tower, as a shout rose from many throats. The men in the forest dashed over the frozen stream to stand in the open before the south-facing door. Two men, weapons in hand, sprang out of the barrier of low-growing bushes edging the stream and attacked the half-dozen warriors at the door. Their rush was ferocious, and loud clangs sounded when their weapons kissed those of their foes.

Okton-iyo heard grunts and moans as the fight raged on.

Those who had begun battering at the door turned to help their fellows, forgetting what they had been doing. Okton-iyo did not forget, crawling from his hut and running on numb feet to reach the door as it began to sag open. Once again his cracked old voice rose in the Song of

Taonhiawagi, for he did not care, now, if anyone saw him. But those battling before the tower did not seem able either to see or hear him.

# CHAPTER TWENTY-FIVE

## A Door Is Bolted

The long wait, locked into that musty tower chamber, was almost Thomas's undoing. He hated being beneath a roof, a matter which his patient wife had long understood, and even a friendly one troubled him. Knowing that he was in the hands of the man who had done away with his daughters, he found that this was almost too much for him.

Athol seemed unconcerned, but Thomas noted that the younger man avoided meeting his eyes and kept staring into the fire with more than natural interest. Noblesse oblige was a matter that he had explained to Thomas when he was a boy. Even then it had seemed to the Falconer's son to be unnatural.

The night was endless. The day following it was even longer, and he tried peering out through the cracks in the nailed shutters, which his and Athol's strongest efforts had failed to open. He kept sane by searching through the cracks in the shutters, scanning narrow slivers of the forest for any sign of life.

The sorcerer sent no food to them, though each had his own supplies in his wallet, so they didn't go hungry. Worse was the thirst that became worse as the day passed. The bucket in the corner was empty, but it had been meant for waste, not water. Some time late in the day Thomas started up, hearing the blast of a hunting horn ring in the distance. He stared at Athol, but the young man looked gloomy and said nothing. Both knew, Thomas understood too well, that Ulric's call was the one they had heard.

By dark, the small amount of wood in the room was all but gone, although they had been miserly with it, for the chimney devoured fuel and let out only skimpy warmth. Once Athol had set the last stick in the heap of coals on the hearth, Thomas stirred and spoke.

"We must try again to escape, Athol. Bad as Ulric manages to be, I feel in my bones that yon wizard is far worse. Night is the time when such magicians do their work, and dark is drawing in. I've no stomach to stay and find out what he wants of us."

The tall man rose from his haunches and stood beside him. "Agreed," said the lazy voice. "I have no confidence in our ability to open either door or window, but that will give us something to do. Perhaps we can shift the door on its hinges and make a crack for a knife-blade to slip through."

But it was no good, and the door seemed as enduring as the tower itself. Once they had exhausted their efforts, they stood in the dying firelight and gazed at each other, their faces pale despite the ruddy coals.

"Thomas, I have led you wrongly," said Athol, his voice sad and quiet. "I never intended to bring you to harm, for you have always been my true friend. Such harm as I have brought you to frightens even me. I intended nothing but good for you and your family. I regret exceedingly that I have caused you to come here and to face what must wait for us this night."

Thomas reached for his hand, and the pair locked grips with desperate intensity. "I'll do my best not to disgrace ye," the poacher managed to say, "though I never got the hang o' this noblesse oblige matter. But you have my word I shall try."

He saw Athol blink hard, as if to keep back tears. He

turned away and stared into the embers in the hearth. Outside it was almost dark, for nothing but blackness marked the cracks through which he had stared.

Time moved slowly, slowly, and he withdrew into his own thoughts, silent in the growing dimness as the last glimmers of fire died from the coals. Then there came the ghost of a sound at the door. Metal whispered against metal as the bolt slid back.

Athol sprang up, silent as a cat, and slid to one side of the door, while Thomas moved cautiously to the other. The latch rose as someone moved it, trying for silence. The door eased open a crack, then a bit more.

Thomas, ready to spring at the sorcerer and throttle him, barehanded if need be, stepped back in shock, for a woman's face shone dimly in the gloom. She put her finger to her lips, signaling silence, and the huntsman nodded. "Qui-et," she said, and something about the sound of the word told him that she was speaking a tongue strange to her. He glanced at Athol, who seemed to think for an instant before nodding decisively. The pair moved toward the door, only to find that their feet, willing though they were, could not carry them past the threshold.

The woman looked back, saw their desperate attempts, and returned. She knelt and felt along the floor, up the frame of the door. Then she stood and chanted in a voice so soft that the strange syllables were lost before they could reach Thomas's ears. Thomas found that he could move, and he followed Athol after her and across the landing. They walked carefully as they moved down the stair behind her, setting their feet near the wall and testing the ancient treads so as to avoid undue noise.

When they reached the space inside the tower door, she paused and stared, as if assessing them. "En-e-mee?" she asked, pointing upward.

Athol bent his proud head before this dark-skinned stranger, half seen in the remnant of light from the guttering torch at the top of the stair. He took her hand into his, as he said, "We are his enemies, yes." He spoke slowly, as if to a child or a foreigner. "He took that one's children. His little ones, you understand?"

Even in the dimness, her eyes flashed as she nodded. "Yes. Some words I have. Go. Out. We make...gawenda... speech?...with that one. Go!"

Thomas had worked on the door as she spoke with Athol, and now he touched the other man's elbow and pointed outward as the door swung back. The sky held a bit of light still along the edges of the western clouds. The tangle of bushes running up the eastern bank of the stream could be seen as a dark blur.

He pointed toward that. "We heard Ulric's horn earlier. He is near, or I'm a fool, and we'd best hide and see who's about before we go openly into the night," he whispered. Athol loosed the woman's hand and they crept into the darkness and found the line of bushes. Behind them, the door opened and closed so quickly that no glimpse of the faint glimmer from the stairwell escaped.

The two moved around the tower. Working his way to the edge of the stream, Thomas turned his attention to the forest on the east, but he could hear nothing there except the hiss of wind on snow and the creaking of snow-burdened branches. When he moved toward the western bank, however, he caught the sound of a careless footstep, crunching into a drift, and a guttural whisper of caution.

Athol, just behind him, touched his elbow. "Ulric," he breathed into his ear, the merest wisp of sound. "Is he then about to attack Lallius? And is he there with his men, though he was supposed to be gone courting?"

They sank into hiding, their faces close together, and Athol continued, "No underling of Ulric's would dare to take it upon himself to stir up this nest of wizardry, I know. Thomas, I feel in my gut that my cousin is out there this moment, waiting to besiege this tower."

Thomas grunted softly. "It may be that he heard some rumor of your return and came post-haste to find you. None of ours in the village would chance letting that slip, but others might have learned of your passing through other places.

"Think you that your cousin might be setting out to rid himself of the two worst burrs beneath his arse at one time? You and Lallius both at once would be a rare feat, and that would be like him."

Now the sky held no streak of light at all, and the night was black. The streak of fire that shot from the wood came as a shocking surprise. It was followed almost at once by a second fire-arrow, which confirmed Thomas's guess. This was Ulric's sort of tactic, without doubt, and the Lord was now attacking the tower, wizard or no wizard. The second arrow found its mark in one of the old shutters, and the ancient wood, even damp with snow, began to smolder and then to burn brightly.

Someone cried out a command, and there came the sound of feet running across the snowy ice of the river. A mailed fist pounded on the heavy door of the tower.

"We must not lose this chance," Athol said into Thomas's ear. "A desperate effort, but we are not unused to those, eh, Thomas? Are you game for it?"

"When have you ever found me lacking?" he grunted, as they rose cautiously in the dark shrubbery and turned toward the attackers.

They sprang onto the rear rank of Ulric's troop, striking them from behind. Two men sank beneath their steel and they leaped over to encounter those now turning, bewildered at the sudden foray, to face them. Now the burning shutter provided light for fighting, and Ulric, his face ruddy in that glow, shouted, recognizing his cousin. He pushed forward between two of his men, his blade ready, and confronted Athol.

"Cousin! I have been searching for you for years now,

and here I have you at last. Now you will die, and I will be troubled no more." He sprang forward, and there came to Thomas's ears the harsh ring of steel on steel.

Thomas held back, allowing the nobles to fight unhindered, but he watched the other men closely, and when one began creeping around to take Athol from the back the huntsman used his long knife to gut the man who had been holding him at bay. Moving aside, he faced the back-stabber and kicked the sword from his hand. His throat was cut before the trooper could cry out.

This left a single man for him to keep busy until Athol could deal with him. Thomas was no gentleman, skilled with the sword; quick and experienced as he might be at rough-and-tumble, he was no match for the nimble blade-play of the one he faced.

He did not notice the opening of the door. Only with a fragment of his mind did he note the reedy voice rising from the forest or see the shape of an ancient man, dressed in strange clothing, as he came walking through the trees.

At that moment, Athol struck deep into Ulric's belly. With an agonized grunt, the Lord sank to his knees, staring up at his victorious cousin with venom in his eyes.

"God's blood and bones! You have killed me, Athol! Never would I have thought you capable, with your pale liver and softness toward the commons, of taking the part of a man. It's of a piece...." but blood gushed from his mouth as he retched, groaned, and fell face-down into the trampled snow.

Thomas, desperately parrying the flashing blade of his opponent with his inadequate knife, saw Athol swing his great blade and sever the Lord's neck, just above the edge of his hauberk.

"You never favored wearing a helm, Cousin," he jeered, as the blade came down. "I thank the Virgin for that!" Then he stood panting, staring down at the dead man, his face grim and striped with sweat and blood.

Thomas's opponent threw down his sword as he saw his master die. He was terribly pale in the light of the burning shutter, as he glanced timidly at his new Lord.

"I now rule here," said Athol. "Take service with me, and I will spare your life. If you do not, I shall let you die here with your former master. Choose, Holt!"

The man sank to his knees and blubbered that he had always thought well of the Lord Athol. Thomas felt sick at his sniveling and turned away. He saw that the door of the tower was now standing wide. Against the snow, down the track beside the river, three shapes were lit by the red light from the shutter as they moved away together.

A fourth figure came after them, erect and wrapped in a silvery fur that shone pale as snow. He was singing, his voice cracked and faded, and the alien strain of a chant came to his ears.

"Look!" Thomas called to Athol, and his new Lord turned. The wailing notes of that song echoed between the forests to east and to west as the group moved southward. Thomas, straining his eyes, realized that he knew the tallest, thinnest shape, wrapped in its black cloak.

"Yon's Lallius!" he said.

Athol grunted agreement. "And the shortest is that woman who loosed us from our prison, but how did she escape from the tower without our seeing her? And who are those other two with her?" Athol's voice was filled with astonishment.

Then the walkers vanished into the darkness beyond the light, leaving Thomas to puzzle over their dreamlike appearance and disappearance for the rest of his life.

# CHAPTER TWENTY-SIX

## Lallius Awakes

The sorcerer had not intended to sleep so long, but something had held him beneath the waters of evil dream, though he struggled to rise and go about his business for the night. He had opened his eyes more than once, but always he had been pulled under again. When his door opened, allowing a frigid draught from the stairwell to rush like an ill tide into his laboratory, he was able to bring himself fully awake at last. He stared up into darkness, but not into silence, for he could hear a confused noise, as if men battled below.

Then the torch from the landing, almost spent, was carried into his room, and he leaped upright, ready to defend this most sacred of his refuges. Once he saw who held the torch, he went still, as if frozen in place. The woman! That thrice-accursed woman who had come through his trap stood there beside his door, her left hand holding the torch high, and behind her was another. A man. They were alike in skin and hair and eyes, for their gazes pinned him fast to the floor, when all his instincts told him to attack them with all his years of hoarded magic.

Even in so unexpected a situation, however, Lallius realized that not a single of his spells had worked as he had intended upon that woman. She had resisted, thwarted, subverted each as he called it to bear upon her. He must not waste his energies upon efforts that could not succeed. The power that shielded her was proof against his spells.

He had nothing to fear, for these people could not escape from his world. Still, he found it in him to wonder if the man had come through in the brief instant in which his door had opened on his last attempt at getting others through from that other world.

His door would not open again without the proper ritual, which he would never consent to perform. So, no matter what they intended, these primitives would be unable to take him far from the base of his power.

As if reading his thought, the woman gestured toward the window, and Lallius, wondering, went and pushed the shutter away. Red light colored the snow below, and men struggled there, the clang of their weapons faint but distinct. What had occurred while he slept that unnatural sleep? He felt the touch of an alien power about him, not to his detriment but very much to his distraction. Someone had sunk him so deeply into slumber that he had lost this great opportunity for which he had worked and studied so hard and so long.

He raised his right hand stiffly before him and began his chant. The fingers began to glow, rivaling the sputtering torch the woman held. The man moved, so suddenly, so lithely that Lallius had no instant in which to move or to think. Then that strong, dark arm was about his throat. A cold stone blade touched his skin, the angled chips forming its edge pushing into the artery at his neck.

A wave of pure terror washed over the wizard. Not since his handling by the guards, back in his own world almost a century ago, had another dared to set his hands on him in such a manner. He stood very still, smelling the odor of wood smoke and oil and strange flesh from the body so close to his own.

The woman stared up at him, her eyes dark pools of shadow, her bronze cheekbones prominent in the torchlight. "You go...with us," she said. "We take...away. Our ionni, our people. You no...keep here. Too much here for you."

The words came awkwardly, but he was amazed that she had comprehended so much in so short a while. He knew just what she meant, and his estimation of her intelligence rose. She knew that if he remained in his own place, surrounded by his equipment, he would try again to find slaves.

Perhaps not in her world, but she could not know that. In her situation, he would, he had to admit as he walked cautiously forward, that knife still too near his throat, have done the same thing himself.

# CHAPTER TWENTY-SEVEN

## A SHORT STEP BETWEEN WORLDS

As soon as Two-Moons fastened the door behind those two they had freed from the tower room, she turned and climbed the stair again. Runs-Bucks waited in the flickering torchlight on the landing, his entire body tense with purpose.

"Is it time now?" he asked, nodding toward that door behind which the sorcerer slept.

"More than time," she whispered, moving to listen at the door. "I feel his wickedness working within him, boiling like a pot into which you drop hot stones. Though he sleeps, still he dreams of doing evil things to people.

"It is time he learns that he cannot make any Onondaga serve him, though he thought, in the beginning, that I might become his slave. We must wake him, but his door is barred within, and we cannot break it down."

Runs Bucks's white teeth showed fleetingly as he smiled. "Do you not recall how we opened that other door? Link hands with me, Two-Moons, and I will see if Taonhiawagi will help me again to make my vision do the work of flesh."

They were still weary from that first use of such power, but she took his hand into hers and leaned against the wall as he began his call upon the Master of Life. It was not so hard, this time, and moving the bolt did not take so long. She heard the slither of metal and he breathed a word into her ear.

The door opened easily to her push, and the two of them entered the room. Lallius's eyes opened, as if with great difficulty, then closed again. But at last they opened wide and he leaped up from his couch. He stared at the pair of them, and Two-Moons could see his chest heaving as he panted. They had surprised and frightened Burning-hand, she knew, yet she also understood that he might be even more dangerous when he was afraid.

She motioned toward the window, and he turned, as if unwilling yet unable to withstand his curiosity, and looked out into the troubled night. When he came away from the opening, his face was pale, his eyes staring. She saw the intention in his eyes before he began to raise that burning hand.

She hissed between her teeth, and Runs-Bucks was a silent breath of air as he passed her and seized the sorcerer from behind, putting his knife to the wizard's throat. When the man went still, she looked up into his face, seeing in his expression the devious process of his thought.

When she spoke, she saw his surprise and felt a grim amusement. He had not expected her to be capable of learning so much, it was obvious. She motioned toward the black cloak, hanging from its peg on the wall, and the man lifted it down and wrapped it about his lanky body. She turned into the room in which she had waited with Runs-Bucks, bringing out the fur cloaks and the bows and bundled arrows, together with her pouch. Two-Moons stared about the tower for an instant, recalling all the strange things that had happened here. Then she shrugged and started down the stair, packs slung from either shoulder, allowing Runs-Bucks to follow the wizard, his knife at the ready.

At the bottom of the stair, she paused to string her bow and nock an arrow, for she could not guess what was happening outside. They might have to fight their way clear of the tower to find the path leading to the doorway into their own world.

Runs-Bucks used that time to bind the hands of Burning-hand and to hobble his ankles, so that he could take only short steps. Another thong went around the thin white neck, secured at its other end to the warrior's waist. Then, his hands free, Runs-Bucks readied his own bow. Clashes and groans from beyond the door told both the Onondaga that the battle still raged outside.

Then, for a moment, the noise quieted, and into the lull came a familiar voice from someplace close at hand, faint, and yet chanting a song that Two-Moons recognized with joy. She gazed up at Runs-Bucks, feeling a shiver of awe.

"Is it Okton-iyo?" she asked. "How did he come to this place, Runs-Bucks? He is singing the Song of Taonhiawagi! That is a great magic! A good omen...."

Weapons crashed together again, as she unbarred the door and peered out through a crack. She saw men lying on the ground, their blood garish in the red light from the burning shutter. Only four still stood, and they did not seem to notice as she and Runs-Bucks herded their prisoner out of the door.

"Hurry!" she said, pushing the sorcerer ahead of her. "The chant is hiding us from those men, I think, though they are also very busy. Go swiftly! You have the talisman ready?"

The warrior touched his pouch and nodded. "It is here. Let us go now as quickly as possible."

As they reached the path beyond the stream, she glanced back at the tower, Behind them, along the path, walked the frail shape of old Okton-iyo, still singing. He did not falter, though his voice was very faint, as he came to join his kinsmen. Those battling about the tower did not seem to see him.

While she watched those fighting at the base of the

structure, Two-Moons saw one man fall beneath the blade of that one who had spoken to her when she freed him. She felt a sudden joy that he had won, for he had spoken gently and his orenda, while alien and rough, had not been evil.

The snow, which seemed to be an ever-present part of this world, began falling again as she trudged after the others along the track through the forest. Big flakes fell slowly, making the air thick and all but hiding the trees.

Two-Moons slowed, feeling her way back through the use of orenda. "I came this way through heavy snow," she said to Runs-Bucks, through the faint sound of Oktoniyo's chant. "Bring out your talisman, Runs-Bucks, for we are not far from the place where I came through the door."

She passed the others, feeling for the precise place that she remembered. Then she stopped and turned. "Feel here, Runs-Bucks. Here is the oak. Now it is time to hold up your key! Lead us home again!"

He handed the talisman to her, and she took it into her hand, feeling a tingle of warmth and energy as it touched her skin. The small pouch almost throbbed against her fingers as she moved steadily forward, feeling the path through her sensing.

She raised her hand, the talisman swinging from its thong as she let it hang from her fingertips. With a feeling of shock, she saw a greenish glimmer begin to form above the path before her. A circle began to glow, and it was familiar and strange. She turned to her companions. "There is the doorway. Can you see it shining amid the snow?"

Runs-Bucks was there, followed by his uncle, and he held the sorcerer firmly by his arm. She half turned to make certain the door was still in place, and then she set a foot through the opening. Feeling firmness beneath her moccasin, she stepped through completely, but she reached back the hand holding the talisman, so as to keep the door intact for the others to follow.

The warrior thrust Burning-hand through the door and came after him quickly. Then came Okton-iyo, and once his foot touched his own world again the chant died away in his throat, and he almost fell. Suddenly he looked even older than he actually was.

Two-Moons brought her hand into the snow-clad wood of elm and maple, and the glimmer of the doorway died away entirely. Burning-hand turned to see the last spark flicker out, and with a yell he leaped toward the place where the door had been.

He jerked free of Runs-Bucks, who had not expected the move, and the thong about his neck pulled tight and snapped. The magician dashed wildly forward, but the passage was gone, and he could not find it again.

He whirled, in a mad flap of black cloak, and seized Two-Moons' hand, which held the talisman. He wrenched at her wrist, trying to take the key, and she fought him grimly, as her companions tried to catch the man's flailing limbs in order to tie the thong about his throat again. But even though his hands were still tied together before him, Burning-hand's fingers were locked about the Dreamer's throat. Two-Moons felt her head swell with trapped blood. She tried to breathe, but there was no air, and she could not even wheeze.

A drum pounded in her body and her head. Bright colors burst behind her eyeballs, as she heard the crack that was her own neck breaking. Then all was gone—the wood, Runs-Bucks, Okton-iyo, and Burning-hand. She floated, bodiless, over a cupped valley.

Having no body, she felt no pain, and she knew neither concern nor despair. As she drifted with the light breeze from the hills beyond the valley, she began to see the sky.

Two moons blossomed there, where sunset dyed the clouds with lavender and gold.

# CHAPTER TWENTY-EIGHT

## THE SLAVE

Lallius felt certain that he would die now. The eyes of the dark-skinned man told him as much, when those irresistible hands caught his body and lifted him from his feet as if he were a child. The iron muscles squeezed until the wizard could not breathe, and he knew that he might well be torn to pieces in the fury of this barbarian.

But the frail old man spoke softly, a single word, and the hands slacked their grip. Lallius slipped to the snow, going to his knees and shuddering convulsively all through his body.

It was not only the death that had stared at him from those dark eyes that shook him. For the first time since he was a child, near two centuries before, he had no sense of the presence of those spirits upon which he had called for assistance through all his long life.

His demons did not exist here. They could not follow him into this world—or would not follow. However it was, they were gone, and he knew that he was powerless forever. He heaved, vomiting into the puddled snow, but they dragged him to his feet and hustled him away through the alien wood. After some time they arrived at a log wall, a palisade of sorts, enclosing a village formed of longhouses built of tree trunks.

The houses were dark against the snow, though flickers of firelight showed through chinks or when someone came or went through one of the skin-closed doors. Toward one of those the big man dragged Lallius. Flinging aside the hide covering the opening, the man moved to the center of the long room and flung the sorcerer onto the packed floor of earth, where a fire burned brightly. An elderly man, his long face wrinkled into a map of line and shadow, stared down at Lallius with surprise but without alarm.

Lallius, pushing himself cautiously to a sitting position, gazed about to find that he sat in the middle of a circle of people around the fire. That group grew larger every moment, as others joined those who stared at him from enigmatic faces.

They talked a great deal, and once in a while he caught a word that the woman had taught him, though he knew too little to make sense of the discussion. After a time his old captor bound him tightly and thrust him into a corner, where a very old woman held a cup of water to his lips and then spat into his face.

It was a very long night for Lallius, filled with discomfort and growing fear. They took him, when morning came, out of the house and into the middle of the village, where a huge bonfire burned. Many men and even a few women took part in the talk there, looking him over, when they looked at all, with anger and contempt in their black eyes.

He began to realize that killing the woman had been a serious mistake. No woman in his own world, except for those of the Royal Family, would have been valued highly enough to make killing her a matter of concern. Even in that other world from which they had brought him, women were held in small esteem.

That woman who had resisted his magic, escaped from his traps, and caused his downfall had been someone of consequence here, it was obvious. What would they do to him for breaking her neck? He shook with fear and cold, for the black cloak they had allowed him to wrap about his naked body, though of wool, was not heavy and never meant for winter wear for long periods out of doors. He managed to tie it about him, as he had done before when escaping from his window in the tower, but that left his long shanks bare to wind and the icy breath of the trampled snow inside the village.

His feet were bruised and his toes felt frozen. One, indeed, was turning black, and he knew he would have to amputate it or he might die. He was more miserable than he had ever dreamed of being in all his long life. Not even when he awaited the headsman had he felt so entirely bereft of hope.

His ordeal did not end with nightfall. He followed his captor back into the longhouse and ate the scraps offered him. Curled in a corner, he wrapped himself in his cloak and shivered the night away, only to be hauled out the next day and stood again before the bonfire.

Days passed slowly, and still those people, snug in their fur robes, talked and talked and talked around their fire. After the third day, however, the discussion ended and two young women were brought into the circle of elders. From gestures and expressions, he had the notion that he was to be given to them as a servant. That, he thought for a moment, would be like setting the wolf to watch the hares. And then he remembered that other woman.

The source of all his troubles had been his capture of that one, and he was less than confident that these two, with their bright eyes and their thin, angry lips, would be any easier to manipulate. There was a look in those flashing eyes that reminded him of the fire in the gaze of the mother of the royal infant, so many years ago. He shivered again, harder. Suddenly, everything was over. Several old women gathered about him, lifted him by his elbows, and carried him away to a corner of the longhouse. There he was put into leather garments, somewhat like those worn by the rest, although entirely too short.

A pair of the soft leather shoes was put onto his painful feet, and a worn hide blanket landed in his arms. Then they pushed him outside into the cold day. The big warrior caught him by the arm and pulled him toward another house. There he shoved him into a partitioned space behind hide hangings, which held a space like a shelf, for sleeping, he thought. The rest of the space was filled with hides and utensils made of pottery and stone and bone and horn.

It was a home, that was clear. The two women entered the cramped place and looked at him disdainfully. One pointed toward a jar and spoke. The other took his arm and jerked him out into the larger house, down the central space and outside. She showed him a spring bubbling through encrusting ice and made motions that told him plainly what his task must be.

They wanted him to bring water to their house. He was to be—the thought astounded him—their slave.

With all his faults, Lallius/Osperre had a sense of humor. Eccentric but keen, it caught him now and he began to laugh. While his new owner stared at him in surprise, he guffawed until his belly hurt.

After a time, he lay down in the snow and rolled, laughing all the while. When he was finished, he filled the pot and carried it back to the longhouse, followed by the puzzled woman who had brought him there. The irony would have been delicious, if he had not been on the receiving end of the joke. He knew that he would grow to regret his long life, perhaps even to shorten it willingly, before all was done.

How many generations of savages must he serve before death freed him of his servitude? There was no humor at all in that thought.

196

# CHAPTER TWENTY-NINE

## A LAST TALK WITH TWO-MOONS

There had been a slight thaw, the sun breaking through and making the snow run and drip into long shards of ice that glittered in the new light. Runs-Bucks, driven by his loneliness, took the opportunity to return to the small dell by the stream, where he found that the new freeze had created a lacework of icicles and frost.

Today was bright though cold, the forest shimmering with brilliant light. Runs-Bucks moved softly into the small space and stood gazing at the frozen stream. When they had talked here, Two-Moons had stood just beside the water, which had bubbled its summer song. He shook himself slightly, as if waking from a dream. He had come with a purpose in his heart, and now he stretched his arms wide and turned his face toward the sky, where thin wisps of cloud promised another storm very soon.

"Two-Moons-In-The-Sky," he called. "Listen to my words! These are the words of your friend and brother, Runs-Bucks-Down. From the Other Place, turn your ear toward me and listen, for I want to tell you what has become of that one who caused your death."

An ice-laden twig snapped, tinkling down through the crystalline ranks below it. Deep in the wood a branch creaked under the weight of deep snow. In the dell there was the feel of waiting.

"Burning-hand, your old enemy and the one who killed you, is now a slave in your sisters' house. We talked of giving him the Honorable Death, but he is unworthy of that. It would give him too much honor. He moaned and wept and struggled in our hands as no brave man would do, and a coward has never been offered that privilege.

"No, we talked for many days, trying to find the most suitable thing for him. Death was too quick and easy, we decided from the start. He must be humbled and made to suffer.

"So we gave him household tasks to do, though he did them very badly for a very long while. Now Laughs-Much makes him sweep out the dirt with bundled twigs and carry offal to the forest, and she only beats him now and then, instead of daily as before."

He closed his eyes and sighed before continuing. "Although I desired to be the one to share your house, that could not be, and though I regretted it to my heart, I understood. You will be pleased to know that I have looked upon your sister Laughs-Much. Though she is not Two-Moons, she is a pleasant woman who works hard and does her tasks well in her fields and her house.

"She has asked me to share her house, and her sister agrees to share it with both of us. I will hunt for us all, and with Burning-hand to do their hardest work and help them with planting, they will be well cared for. If we should have a daughter, she will, we hope, be much like you. We shall comfort each other for your loss and remember you with affection all our lives."

Again he closed his eyes. When he opened them again, he said, "Odatsehe has been shown a dream, which revealed to him many doors and windows opening into our forest over the long years.

"Through those have looked the False-Faces, which have troubled and sickened our people. May Taonhiawagi

198

stop all such doors and prevent such faces from looking again into our forest. With Burning-hand removed from his own place, this may become true."

The harsh cry of a crow rasped from the distance, echoing among the icy trees. Runs-Bucks lowered his arms and looked at the blaze of ice dripping from the walls of the dell.

"Farewell, Two-Moons, sister, warrior, and friend. Dreamer you were, to the great good of our people. Without you, we might all have been drawn through that ghost-door into the terrible world we both know. Even now we might serve Burning-hand as his slaves, without hope of escape, living beneath the threat of his wicked magics.

"Hunt well in the forests of Aireskoi. Rest at the feet of Taonhiawagi. We will not forget you!"

The crow called again, and Runs-Bucks turned to climb up the path into the dell. Beyond rose the white reaches of their own familiar forest.

The clan and the tribe were free, prospering even in this cold winter. He would see to her sisters, and all their children would know the name of their aunt. Two-Moons-In-The-Sky would never be forgotten so long as the Onondaga of their village endured.

# AUTHOR'S NOTE

Although the Iroquoian people of the era of the League of the Longhouse were no more saintly than any other people have ever been, they were, when contrasted with the barbarian Europeans who invaded their continent, marvels of enlightenment. At a time when religion was used as an excuse for war and torture and murder, and when most of any "civilized" population existed in abject poverty and misery, those in the confederated tribes lived far more civilized lives than most of the population of Europe or Asia could boast for many generations.

According to early Jesuits who went into their territory to convert the "heathen" of the Kanonsionni, the members of the League of the Longhouse had no need for charity. Every individual was cared for, old or young, widowed or orphaned or elderly.

No one was rich, for those possessing extra crops or game or fish contributed to those who needed help. If such a person did not, he was scorned and shunned. Wealth did not exist, and the needs of life were pretty evenly distributed.

Personal autonomy was almost complete. A chief or sachem did not dictate to his people as they went about their lives. That chief was chosen by the Matriarchs of the tribe, to be elder and counselor and wise man. If he did not serve well, the old women could remove their choice and find another and better one.

Though incoming Europeans saw women toiling in the fields and thought them to be the sort of oppressed females they knew at home, the truth was that those fields belonged to the women who worked them. Indeed, women of the Iroquoian tribes owned the houses as well. Warriors owned only their clothing and their weapons, and lived in their wives' homes, rather than the reverse.

Although some of their customs struck European sensibilities as cruel and barbaric, when compared to the Inquisition and to the tortures imposed under the legal systems in Europe, as well as to the general cruelty of noble to commoner, those were not nearly as dreadful as they seemed. The Honorable Death, involving torture enduring for the longest possible span of time, was a case in point.

Such a death was a great honor, offered only to those distinguishing themselves in battle against the tribe. When there was room to incorporate such captives into the group, that was often done, but when the population was at its limit, the Honorable Death was the alternative.

Those so honored endured the torture stoically and, in the intervals for rest and refreshment, laughed and joked with their torturers. Those showing the most courage were often ritually eaten, in order to infuse their bravery through the tribe.

The torture was terrible, but seldom did it approach the intensity or the venality of that imposed by the Church during the Inquisition.

Whites who witnessed (or endured) such matters were shocked and appalled. The similarity to the ritual cannibalism of Christianity never entered the minds of those who deplored its use by the Indian cultures.

Considering the filth, cruelty, and oppression imposed upon (and sometimes by) our European ancestors, we might do well to reconsider our attitudes toward the ways of those people they considered vermin and tried vigorously to destroy. While it is traditional to think of the influx of Europeans as civilization entering this barbaric continent, it might be more accurate to think of that as the reverse.

In the case of America, the barbarians won.

## ONONDAGA-IROQUOIAN WORDS AND NAMES

Ahta—shoe
Aksen—bad or ugly
Ase—new
Gawenda—speech, talk
Ikiaks—(verb) I cut
Iyo—good, beautiful
Karenna—hymn or song
Kayanerenh—peace
Kowa—great
Okonha—son
Okonwe—man
Wakonnyh—woman

Names:
Aireskoi—Guide and guarding spirit of hunters
Aronhia—Cloud
Ase-karenna—New-Song
Ayonhwatha—He-Who-Seeks-Wampum
Iyo-Wakonnyh—Good Woman
Kowa-Okonha—Great Son
Odatsehe—Quiver-Bearer
Okton-iyo—Beautiful Spirit
Taonhiawagi—Master of Life, chief of the gods
Kanonsionni—League of the Longhouse (parts of the Constitution of the United States are based directly upon the treaty uniting the League); included among the tribes in that confederation were the Lenni-Lenape (Delaware) and the Nihatientakona, or Oneida, who are referred to herein.

# ABOUT THE AUTHOR

The author of sixty-two books, more than forty of them published commercially, **Ardath Mayhar** began her career in the early eighties with science fiction novels from Doubleday and TSR. Atheneum published several of her young adult and children's novels. Changing focus, she wrote westerns (as **Frank Cannon**) and mountain man novels (as **John Killdeer**), four prehistoric Indian books under her own name, and historical western *High Mountain Winter* under the byline **Frances Hurst**.

Recently she has been working with on-line publishers. *A Road of Stars* was her first original novel to appear in print-on-demand format. Many of her out-of-print titles are now available from e-publishers fictionwise.com and renebooks.com; many other novels are being published by the Borgo Press Imprint of Wildside Press and Amazon.com.

Now in her seventies, Mayhar was widowed in 1999, after forty-one years of marriage, and has four grown sons. She now works at home, writing short fiction and nonfiction, and doing book doctoring professionally. Her web pages can be found at:

w2.netdot.com/ardathm/ and
http://ofearna.us/ books/mayhar.html

www.ingramcontent.com/pod-product-compliance
Lightning Source LLC
Chambersburg PA
CBHW032006240626
47153CB00003B/1141